What I Didn't See

What I Didn't See

and Other Stories

Karen Joy Fowler

Small Beer Press
Easthampton, MA

Small Beer Press
150 Pleasant Street #306
Easthampton, MA 01027
www.smallbeerpress.com
info@smallbeerpress.com

Distributed to the trade by Consortium.

Library of Congress Cataloging-in-Publication Data

Library of Congress Cataloging-in-Publication Data

Fowler, Karen Joy.
  What I didn't see : and other stories / Karen Joy Fowler. -- 1st ed.
    p. cm.
  ISBN 978-1-931520-68-3 (alk. paper)
  I. Title.
  PS3556.0844fi47 2010
  813'.54--DC22

2010025911

First edition 1 2 3 4 5 6 7 8 9

Text set in Centaur.

Printed on 60-lb. 30% recycled paper by Thomson-Shore in Dexter, Michigan.
Cover art © 2010 by Erica Harris.
Author photo © Beth Gwinn.

Contents

For my dad, who generally makes an appearance

The Pelican Bar

For her birthday, Norah got a Pink CD from the twins, a book about vampires from her grown-up sister, *High School Musical 2* from her grandma (which Norah might have liked if she'd been turning ten instead of fifteen), an iPod shuffle plus an Ecko Red T-shirt and two-hundred-dollar darkwash Seven Jeans—the most expensive clothes Norah had ever owned—from her mother and father.

Not a week earlier, her mother had said it was a shame birthdays came whether you deserved them or not. She'd said she was dog-tired of Norah's disrespect, her ingratitude, her filthy language—as if fucking was just another word for *very*—fucking this and fucking that, fucking hot and fucking unfair and you have to be fucking kidding me.

And then there were a handful of nights when Norah didn't come home and turned off her phone so they all thought she was in the city in the apartment of some man she'd probably met on the internet and probably dead.

And then there were the horrible things she'd written about both her mother and father on Facebook.

And now they had to buy her presents?

I don't see that happening, Norah's mother had said.

So it was all a big surprise, and there was even a party. Her parents didn't approve of Norah's friends (and mostly didn't know who

Karen Joy Fowler

they were), so the party was just family. Norah's big sister brought the new baby, who yawned and hiccoughed and whose scalp was scaly with cradle cap. There was barbecued chicken and ears of corn cooked in milk, an ice-cream cake with pralines and roses, and everyone, even Norah, was really careful and nice except for Norah's grandma, who had a fight in the kitchen with Norah's mother that stopped the minute Norah entered. Her grandmother gave Norah a kiss, wished her a happy birthday, and left before the food was served.

The party went late, and Norah's mother said they'd clean up in the morning. Everyone left or went to bed. Norah made a show of brushing her teeth, but she didn't undress, because Enoch and Kayla had said they'd come by, which they did, just before midnight. Enoch climbed through Norah's bedroom window, and then he tiptoed downstairs to the front door to let Kayla in, because she was already too trashed for the window. "Your birthday's not over yet!" Enoch said, and he'd brought Norah some special birthday shrooms called hawk's eyes. Half an hour later, the whole bedroom took a little skip sideways and broke open like an egg. Blue light poured over everything, and Norah's Care Bear, Milo, had a luminous blue aura, as if he were Yoda or something. Milo told Norah to tell Enoch she loved him, which made Enoch laugh.

They took more of the hawk's eyes, so Norah was still tripping the next morning when a man and a woman came into her bedroom, pulled her from her bed, and forced her onto her feet while her mother and father watched. The woman had a hooked nose and slightly protuberant eyeballs. Norah looked into her face just in time to see the fast retraction of a nictitating membrane. "Look at her eyes," she said, only the words came out of the woman's mouth instead of Norah's. "Look at her eyes," the woman said. "She's high as a kite."

Norah's mother collected clothes from the floor and the chair in the bedroom. "Put these on," she told Norah, but Norah couldn't find the sleeves, so the men left the room while her mother dressed her. Then the man and woman took her down the stairs and out the front door to a car so clean and black that clouds rolled across the hood. Norah's father put a suitcase in the trunk, and when he slammed it shut, the noise Norah heard was the last note in a Sunday school choir: the *men* part of *amen*, sung in many voices.

The music was calming. Her parents had been threatening to ship her off to boarding school for so long she'd stopped hearing it. Even now she thought that they were maybe all just trying to scare her, would drive her around for a bit and then bring her back, lesson learned, and this helped for a minute or two. Then she thought her mother wouldn't be crying in quite the way she was crying if it was all for show. Norah tried to grab her mother's arm, but missed. "Please," she started, "don't make me," but before she got the words out the man had leaned in to take them. "Don't make me hurt you," he said in a tiny whisper that echoed in her skull. He handcuffed Norah to the seat belt because she was struggling. His mouth looked like something drawn onto his face with a charcoal pen.

"This is only because we love you," Norah's father said. "You were on a really dangerous path."

"This is the most difficult thing we've ever done," said Norah's mother. "Please be a good girl, and then you can come right home."

The man with the charcoal mouth and the woman with the nictitating eyelids drove Norah to an airport. They showed the woman at the ticket counter Norah's passport, and then they all got on a plane together, the woman in the window seat, the man, the aisle, and Norah in the middle. Sometime during the flight, Norah came down, and the man beside her had an ordinary face and the woman had ordinary eyes, but Norah was still on a plane with nothing beneath her but ocean.

While this was happening, Norah's mother drove to the mall. She had cried all morning, and now she was returning the iPod shuffle to the Apple store and the expensive clothes to Nordstrom's. She had all her receipts, and everything still had the tags, plus she was sobbing intermittently, but uncontrollably, so there was no problem getting her money back.

Norah's new home was an old motel. She arrived after dark, the sky above pinned with stars and the road so quiet she could hear a bubbling chorus of frogs and crickets. The man held her arm and walked just fast enough to make Norah stumble. He let her fall onto one knee. The ground was asphalt covered with a grit that stuck in her skin and couldn't be brushed off. She was having trouble believing she was here. She was having trouble remembering the plane. It was a bad trip, a bad dream, as if she'd gone to bed in her bedroom as usual and awakened here. Her drugged-up visions of eyelids and mouths were forgotten; she was left with only a nagging suspicion she couldn't track back. But she didn't feel like a person being punished for bad behavior. She felt like an abductee.

An elderly woman in a flowered caftan met them at a chain-link gate. She unlocked it, and the man pushed Norah through without a word. "My suitcase," Norah said to the man, but he was already gone.

"Now I am your mother," the woman told Norah. She was very old, face like a crumpled leaf. "But not like your other mother. Two things different. One: I don't love you. Two: when I tell you what to do, you do it. You call me Mama Strong." Mama Strong stooped a little so she and Norah were eye to eye. Her pupils were tiny black beads. "You sleep now. We talk tomorrow."

They climbed an outside stairway, and Norah had just a glimpse of the moon-streaked ocean on the other side of the chainlink. Mama Strong took Norah to Room 217. Inside, ten girls were already in bed, the floor nearly covered with mattresses, only narrow channels of brown rug between. The light in the ceiling was on, but the girls' eyes were shut. A second old woman sat on a stool in the corner. She was sucking loudly on a red lollipop. "I don't have my toothbrush," Norah said.

"I didn't say brush your teeth," said Mama Strong. She gave Norah a yellow T-shirt, gray sweatpants, and plastic flip-flops, took her to the bathroom and waited for Norah to use the toilet, wash her face with tap water, and change. Then she took the clothes Norah had arrived in and went away.

The old woman pointed with her lollipop to an empty mattress, thin wool blanket folded at the foot. Norah lay down, covered herself with the blanket. The room was stuffy, warm, and smelled of the bodies in it. The mattress closest to Norah's belonged to a skinny black girl with a scabbed nose and a bad cough. Norah knew she was awake because of the coughing. "I'm Norah," she whispered, but the old woman in the corner hissed and clapped her hands. It took Norah a long time to realize that no one was ever going to turn off the light.

Three times during the night she heard someone screaming. Other times she thought she heard the ocean, but she was never sure; it could have been a furnace or a fan.

In the morning, the skinny girl told Mama Strong that Norah had talked to her. The girl earned five points for this, which was enough to be given her hairbrush.

"I said no talking," Mama Strong told Norah.

"No, you didn't," said Norah.

"Who is telling the truth? You or me?" asked Mama Strong.

Norah, who hadn't eaten since the airplane or brushed her teeth in twenty-four hours, had a foul taste in her mouth like rotting eggs. Even so, she could smell the onions on Mama Strong's breath. "Me," said Norah.

She lost ten points for the talking and thirty for the talking back. This put her, on her first day, at minus forty. At plus ten she would have earned her toothbrush; at plus twenty, her hairbrush.

Mama Strong said that no talking was allowed anywhere—points deducted for talking—except at group sessions, where talking was required—points deducted for no talking. Breakfast was cold hard toast with canned peaches—points deducted for not eating—after which Norah had her first group session.

Mama Strong was her group leader. Norah's group was the girls from Room 217. They were, Norah was told, her new family. Her family name was Power. Other families in the hotel were named Dignity, Consideration, Serenity, and Respect. These were, Mama Strong said, not so good as family names. Power was the best.

There were boys in the west wings of the motel, but they wouldn't ever be in the yard at the same time as the girls. Everyone ate together, but there was no talking while eating, so they wouldn't be getting to know each other; anyway, they were all very bad boys. There was no reason to think about them at all, Mama Strong said.

She passed each of the Power girls a piece of paper and a pencil. She told them to write down five things about themselves that were true.

Norah thought about Enoch and Kayla, whether they knew where she had gone, what they might try to do about it. What she would do if it were them. She wrote: *I am a good friend. I am fun to be with.* Initially that was a single entry. Later when time ran out, she came back and made it two. She thought about her parents. *I am a picky eater*, she wrote on their behalf. She couldn't afford to be angry with them, not until she was home again. A mistake had been made. When her parents realized the kind of place this was, they would come and get her.

I am honest. I am stubborn, she wrote, because her mother had always said so. How many times had Norah heard how her mother spent eighteen hours in labor and finally had a C-section just because Fetal Norah wouldn't tuck her chin to clear the pubic bone. "If I'd known her then like I know her now," Norah's mother used to say, "I'd have gone straight to the C-section and spared myself the labor. 'This child is never going to tuck her chin,' I'd have said."

And then Norah scratched out the part about being stubborn, because she had never been so angry at her parents and she didn't want to give her mother the satisfaction. Instead she wrote, *Nobody knows who I really am.*

They were all to read their lists aloud. Norah was made to go first. Mama Strong sucked loudly through her teeth at number four. "Already this morning, Norah has lied to me two times," she told the group. "'I am honest' is the third lie today."

The girls were invited to comment. They did so immediately and with vigor. Norah seemed very stuck on herself, said a white girl with severe acne on her cheeks and chin. A red-haired girl with a freckled neck and freckled arms said that there was no evidence of Norah taking responsibility for anything. She agreed with the first girl. Norah was very stuck-up. The skinny girl with the cough said that no one honest ended up here. None of them were honest, but at least she was honest enough to admit it.

"I'm here by mistake," said Norah.

"Lie number four." Mama Strong reached over and took the paper, her eyes like stones. "*I* know who you really are," she said. "*I* know how you think. You think, how do I get out of here?

"*You* never will. The only way out is to be different. Change. Grow." She tore up Norah's list. "Only way is to be someone else completely. As long as some tiny place inside is still you, you will never leave."

The other girls took turns reading from their lists. "I am ungrateful," one of them had written. "I am a liar," read another. "I am still carrying around my bullshit," read the girl with the cough. "I am a bad person." "I am a bad daughter."

—⁊⁊—

It took Norah three months to earn enough points to spend an afternoon outside. She stood blinking in the sun, watching a line of birds thread the sky above her. She couldn't see the ocean, but there was a breeze that brought the smell of salt.

Later she got to play kickball with the other Power girls in the old, drained motel pool. No talking, so they played with a silent ferocity, slamming each other into the pool walls until every girl was bleeding from the nose or the knee or somewhere.

After group there were classes. Norah would be given a lesson with a multiple-choice exercise. Some days it was math, some days history, geography, literature. At the end of an hour someone on staff would check her answers against a key. There was no instruction, and points were deducted for wrong answers. One day the lesson was the Frost poem "The Road Not Taken," which was not a hard lesson, but Norah got almost everything wrong, because the staff member was using the wrong key. Norah said so, and she lost points for her poor score, but also for the talking.

It took eleven months for Norah to earn enough points to write her parents. She'd known Mama Strong or someone else on staff would read the letter so she wrote it carefully. "Please let me come home. I promise to do whatever you ask and I think you can't know much about this place. I am sick a lot from the terrible food and have a rash on my legs from bug bites that keeps getting worse. I've lost weight. Please come and get me. I love you. Norah."

"So manipulative," Mama Strong had said. "So dishonest and manipulative." But she put the letter into an envelope and stamped it.

If the letter was dishonest, it was only by omission. The food here was not only terrible, it was unhealthy, often rotting, and there was never enough of it. Meat was served infrequently, so the students, hungry enough to eat anything, were always sick after. No more than three minutes every three hours could be spent on the toilet; there were always students whose legs were streaked with diarrhea. There was no medical care. The bug bites came from her mattress.

Sometimes someone would vanish. This happened to two girls in the Power family. One of them was the girl with the acne; her name was Kelsey. One of them was Jetta, a relatively new arrival. There was no explanation; since no one was allowed to talk, there was no speculation. Mama Strong had said if they earned a hundred points they could leave. Norah tried to remember how many points she'd seen Kelsey get; was it possible she'd had a hundred? Not possible that Jetta did.

The night Jetta disappeared, there was a bloody towel in the corner of the shower. Not just stained with blood, soaked with it. It stayed in the corner for three days until someone finally took it away.

A few weeks before her birthday, Norah lost all her accumulated points, forty-five of them, for not going deep in group session. By then Norah had no deep left. She was all surface—skin rashes, eye infections, aching teeth, constant hunger, stomach cramps. The people in her life—the ones Mama Strong wanted to know everything about—had dimmed in her memory along with everything else—school, childhood, all the fights with her parents, all the Christmases, the winters, the summers, her fifteenth birthday. Her friends went first and then her family.

The only things she could remember clearly were those things she'd shared in group. Group session demanded ever more intimate, more humiliating, more secret stories. Soon it seemed as if nothing had ever happened to Norah that wasn't shameful and painful. Worse, her most secret shit was still found wanting, not sufficiently revealing, dishonest.

Norah turned to vaguely remembered plots from after-school specials until one day the story she was telling was recognized by the freckled girl, Emilene was her name, who got twenty whole points for calling Norah on it.

There was a punishment called the TAP, the Think Again Position. Room 303 was the TAP room. It smelled of unwashed bodies and was crawling with ants. A student sent to the TAP was forced to lie facedown on the bare floor. Every three hours, a shift in position was allowed. A student who moved at any other time was put in restraint. Restraint meant that one staff member would set a knee on the student's spine. Others would pull the student's arms and legs back and up as far as they could go and then just a little bit farther. Many times a day, screaming could be heard in Room 303.

For lying in group session, Norah was sent to the TAP. She would be released, Mama Strong, said, when she was finally ready to admit that she was here as a result of her own decisions. Mama Strong was sick of Norah's games. Norah lasted two weeks.

"You have something to say?" Mama Strong was smoking a small hand-rolled cigarette that smelled of cinnamon. Smoke curled from her nostrils, and her fingers were stained with tobacco or coffee or dirt or blood.

"I belong here," Norah said.

"No mistake?"

"No."

"Just what you deserve?"

"Yes."

"Say it."

"Just what I deserve."

"Two weeks is nothing," Mama Strong said. "We had a girl three years ago, did eighteen."

Although it was the most painful, the TAP was not, to Norah's mind, the worst part. The worst part was the light that stayed on all night. Norah had not been in the dark for one single second since she arrived. The no dark was making Norah crazy. Her voice in group no longer sounded like her voice. It hurt to use it, hurt to hear it.

Her voice had betrayed her, telling Mama Strong everything until there was nothing left inside Norah that Mama Strong hadn't pawed through, like a shopper at a flea market. Mama Strong knew exactly who Norah was, because Norah had told her. What Norah needed was a new secret.

For her sixteenth birthday, she got two postcards. "We came all this way only to learn you're being disciplined and we can't see you. We don't want to be harsh on your birthday of all days, but honest to Pete, Norah, when are you going to have a change of attitude? Just imagine how disappointed we are." The handwriting was her father's, but the card had been signed by her mother and father both.

The other was written by her mother. "Your father said as long as we're here we might as well play tourist. So now we're at a restaurant in the middle of the ocean. Well, maybe not the exact middle, but a long ways out! The restaurant is up on stilts on a sandbar and you can only get here by boat! We're eating a fish right off the line! All the food is so good, we envy you living here! Happy birthday, darling! Maybe next year we can celebrate your birthday here together. I will pray for that!" Both postcards had a picture of the ocean restaurant. It was called the Pelican Bar.

Her parents had spent five days only a few miles away. They'd swum in the ocean, drunk mai tais and mojitos under the stars, fed bits of bread to the gulls. They'd gone up the river to see the crocodiles and shopped for presents to take home. They were genuinely sorry about Norah; her mother had cried the whole first day and often after. But this sadness was heightened by guilt. There was no denying that they were happier at home without her. Norah had been a constant drain, a constant source of tension and despair. Norah left and peace arrived. The twins had never been difficult,

Karen Joy Fowler

but Norah's instructive disappearance had improved even their good behavior.

Norah is on her mattress in Room 217 under the overhead light, but she is also at a restaurant on stilts off the coast. She is drinking something made with rum. The sun is shining. The water is blue and rocking like a cradle. There is a breeze on her face.

Around the restaurant, nets and posts have been sunk into the sandbar. Pelicans sit on these or fly or sometimes drop into the water with their wings closed, heavy as stones. Norah wonders if she could swim all the way back in to shore. She's a good swimmer, or used to be, but this is merely hypothetical. She came by motorboat, trailing her hand in the water, and will leave the same way. Norah wipes her mouth with her hand, and her fingers taste of salt.

She buys a postcard. *Dear Norah,* she writes. *You could do the TAP better now. Maybe not for eighteen weeks, but probably more than two. Don't ever tell Mama Strong about the Pelican Bar, no matter what.*

For her sixteenth birthday what Norah got was the Pelican Bar.

Norah's seventeenth birthday passed without her noticing. She'd lost track of the date; there was just a morning when she suddenly thought that she must be seventeen by now. There'd been no card from her parents, which might have meant they hadn't sent one, but probably didn't. Their letters were frequent, if peculiar. They seemed to think there was water in the pool, fresh fruit at lunchtime. They seemed to think she had counselors and teachers and friends. They'd even made reference to college prep. Norah knew that someone on staff was writing and signing her name. It didn't matter. She could hardly remember her parents, didn't expect to ever see them again. Since "come and get me" hadn't worked, she had nothing further to say to them. Fine with her if someone else did.

One of the night women, one of the women who sat in the corner and watched while they slept, was younger than the others, with her hair in many braids. She took a sudden dislike to Norah. Norah had no idea why; there'd been no incident, no exchange, just an evening when the woman's eyes locked onto Norah's face and filled with poison. The next day she followed Norah through the halls and lobby, mewing at her like a cat. This went on until everyone on staff was mewing at Norah. Norah lost twenty points for it. Worse, she found it impossible to get to the Pelican Bar while everyone was mewing at her.

But even without Norah going there, Mama Strong could tell that she had a secret. Mama Strong paid less attention to the other girls and more to Norah, pushing and prodding in group, allowing the mewing even from the other girls, and sending Norah to the TAP again and again. Norah dipped back into minus points. Her hairbrush and her toothbrush were taken away. Her time in the shower was cut from five minutes to three. She had bruises on her thighs and a painful spot on her back where the knee went during restraint.

After several months without, she menstruated. The blood came in clots, gushes that soaked into her sweatpants. She was allowed to get up long enough to wash her clothes, but the blood didn't come completely out and the sweatpants weren't replaced. A man came and mopped the floor where Norah had to lie. It smelled strongly of piss when he was done.

More girls disappeared, until Norah noticed that she'd been there longer than almost anyone in the Power family. A new girl arrived and took the mattress and blanket Kimberly had occupied. The new girl's name was Chloe. The night she arrived, she spoke to Norah. "How long have you been here?" she asked. Her eyes were red and swollen, and she had a squashed kind of nose. She wasn't able to hold still; she jabbered about her meds which she hadn't taken and needed to; she rocked on the mattress from side to side.

"The new girl talked to me last night," Norah told Mama Strong in the morning. Chloe was a born victim, gave off the victim vibe. She was so weak, it was like a superpower. The kids at her school had bullied her, she said in group session, like this would be news to anyone.

"Maybe you ask for it," Emilene suggested.

"Why don't you take responsibility?" Norah said. "Instead of blaming everyone else."

"You will learn to hold still," Mama Strong told her and had the girls put her in restraint themselves. Norah's was the knee in her back.

Then Mama Strong told them all to make a list of five reasons they'd been sent here. "I am a bad daughter," Norah wrote. "I am still carrying around my bullshit. I am ungrateful." And then her brain snapped shut like a clamshell so she couldn't continue.

"There is something else you want to say." Mama Strong stood in front of her, holding the incriminating paper, two reasons short of the assignment, in her hand.

She was asking for Norah's secret. She was asking about the Pelican Bar. "No," said Norah. "It's just that I can't think."

"Tell me." The black beads of Mama Strong's eyes became pinpricks. "Tell me. Tell me." She stepped around Norah's shoulder so that Norah could smell onion and feel a cold breath on her neck, but couldn't see her face.

"I don't belong here," Norah said. She was trying to keep the Pelican Bar. To do that, she had to give Mama Strong something else. There was probably a smarter plan, but Norah couldn't think of anything. "Nobody belongs here," she said. "This isn't a place where humans belong."

"You are human, but not me?" Mama Strong said. Mama Strong

had never touched Norah. But her voice coiled like a spring; she made Norah flinch. Norah felt her own piss on her thighs.

"Maybe so," Mama Strong said. "Maybe I'll send you somewhere else then. Say you want that. Ask me for it. Say it and I'll do it."

Norah held her breath. In that instant, her brain produced the two missing reasons. "I am a liar," she said. She heard her own desperation. "I am a bad person."

There was a silence, and then Norah heard Chloe saying she wanted to go home. Chloe clapped her hands over her mouth. Her talking continued, only now no one could make out the words. Her head nodded like a bobblehead dog on a dashboard.

Mama Strong turned to Chloe. Norah got sent to the TAP, but not to Mama Strong's someplace else.

After that, Mama Strong never again seemed as interested in Norah. Chloe hadn't learned yet to hold still, but Mama Strong was up to the challenge. When Norah was seventeen, the gift she got was Chloe.

One day, Mama Strong stopped Norah on her way to breakfast. "Follow me," she said, and led Norah to the chain-link fence. She unlocked the gate and swung it open. "You can go now." She counted out fifty dollars. "You can take this and go. Or you can stay until your mother and father come for you. Maybe tomorrow. Maybe next week. You go now, you get only as far as you get with fifty dollars."

Norah began to shake. This, she thought, was the worst thing done to her yet. She took a step toward the gate, took another. She didn't look at Mama Strong. She saw that the open gate was a trick, which made her shaking stop. She was not fooled. Norah would never be allowed to walk out. She took a third step and a fourth. "You don't belong here," Mama Strong said with contempt, as if there'd been a

Karen Joy Fowler

test and Norah had flunked it. Norah didn't know if this was because she'd been too compliant or not compliant enough.

And then Norah was outside and Mama Strong was closing and locking the gate behind her.

Norah walked in the sunlight down a paved road dotted with potholes and the smashed skins of frogs. The road curved between weeds taller than Norah's head, bushes with bright orange flowers. Occasionally a car went by, driven very fast.

Norah kept going. She passed stucco homes, some small stores. She saw cigarettes and muumuus for sale, large avocados, bunches of small bananas, liquor bottles filled with dish soap, posters for British ale. She thought about buying something to eat, but it seemed too hard, would require her to talk. She was afraid to stop walking. It was very hot on the road in the sun. A pack of small dogs followed her briefly and then ran back to wherever they'd come from.

She reached the ocean and walked into the water. The salt stung the rashes on her legs, the sores on her arms, and then it stopped stinging. The sand was brown, the water blue and warm. She'd forgotten about the fifty dollars though she was still holding them in her hand, now soaked and salty.

There were tourists everywhere on the beach, swimming, lying in the sun with daiquiris and ice-cream sandwiches and salted oranges. She wanted to tell them that, not four miles away, children were being starved and terrified. She couldn't remember enough about people to know if they'd care. Probably no one would believe her. Probably they already knew.

She waded in to shore and walked farther. It was so hot, her clothes dried quickly. She came to a river and an open-air market. A young man with a scar on his cheek approached her. She recognized him. On two occasions, he'd put her in restraint. Her heart began to knock against her lungs. The air around her went black.

"Happy birthday," he said.

He came swimming back into focus, wearing a bright plaid shirt, smiling so his lip rose like a curtain over his teeth. He stepped toward her; she stepped away. "Your birthday, yes?" he said. "Eighteen?" He bought her some bananas, but she didn't take them.

A woman behind her was selling beaded bracelets, peanuts, and puppies. She waved Norah over. "True," she said to Norah. "At eighteen, they have to let you go. The law says." She tied a bracelet onto Norah's wrist. How skinny Norah's arm looked in it. "A present for your birthday," the woman said. "How long were you there?"

Instead of answering, Norah asked for directions to the Pelican Bar. She bought a T-shirt, a skirt, and a cola. She drank the cola, dressed in the new clothes and threw away the old. She bought a ticket on a boat—ten dollars it cost her to go, ten more to come back. There were tourists, but no one sat anywhere near her.

The boat dropped her, along with the others, twenty feet or so out on the sandbar, so that she walked the last bit through waist-high water. She was encircled by the straight, clean line of the horizon, the whole world spinning around her, flat as a plate. The water was a brilliant, sun-dazzled blue in every direction. She twirled slowly, her hands floating, her mind flying until it was her turn on the makeshift ladder of planks and branches and her grip on the wood suddenly anchored her. She climbed into the restaurant in her dripping dress.

She bought a postcard for Chloe. "On your eighteenth birthday, come here," she wrote, "and eat a fish right off the line. I'm sorry about everything. I'm a bad person."

She ordered a fish for herself, but couldn't finish it. She sat for hours, feeling the floor of the bar rocking beneath her, climbing down the ladder into the water and up again to dry in the warm air. She never wanted to leave this place that was the best place in the world, even more beautiful than she'd imagined. She fell asleep on the restaurant bench and didn't wake up until the last boat was going to shore and someone shook her arm to make sure she was on it.

When Norah returned to shore, she saw Mama Strong seated in an outdoor bar at the edge of the market on the end of the dock. The sun was setting and dark coming on. Mama Strong was drinking something that could have been water or could have been whiskey. The glass was colored blue, so there was no way to be sure. She saw Norah getting off the boat. There was no way back that didn't take Norah toward her.

"You have so much money, you're a tourist?" Mama Strong asked. "Next time you want to eat, the money is gone. What then?"

Two men were playing the drums behind her. One of them began to sing. Norah recognized the tune—something old that her mother had liked—but not the words.

"Do you think I'm afraid to go hungry?" Norah said.

"So. We made you tougher. Better than you were. But not tough enough. Not what we're looking for. You go be whatever you want now. Have whatever you want. We don't care."

What did Norah want to be? Clean. Not hungry. Not hurting. What did she want to have? She wanted to sleep in the dark. Already there was one bright star in the sky over the ocean.

What else? She couldn't think of a thing. Mama Strong had said Norah would have to change, but Norah felt that she'd vanished instead. She didn't know who she was anymore. She didn't know anything at all. She fingered the beaded bracelet on her wrist. "When I run out of money," she said, "I'll ask someone to help me. And someone will. Maybe not the first person I ask. But someone." Maybe it was true.

"Very pretty." Mama Strong looked into her blue glass, swirled whatever was left in it, tipped it down her throat. "You're wrong about humans, you know," she said. Her tone was conversational. "Humans do everything we did. Humans do more."

Two men came up behind Norah. She whirled, sure that they were here for her, sure that she'd be taken, maybe back, maybe to Mama Strong's more horrible someplace else. But the men walked right past her, toward the drummers. They walked right past her and as they walked, they began to sing. Maybe they were human and maybe not.

"Very pretty world," said Mama Strong.

Booth's Ghost

One:

I have that within which passeth show . . .

On November 25, 1864, Edwin Booth gave a benefit performance of *Julius Caesar*. One night only, in the Winter Garden Theater in New York City, all profits to fund the raising of a statue of Shakespeare in Central Park. Edwin played the role of Brutus; his older brother, Junius, was Cassius; his younger, John Wilkes, was Mark Antony. The best seats went for as much as five dollars, and their mother and sister Asia were in the audience, flushed with pride.

Act 2, scene 1. Brutus' orchard. Fire engines could be heard outside the theater, and four firemen came into the lobby. The audience began to buzz and shift in their seats. Brutus stepped forward into the foot-lights. "Everything is all right," he told them. "Please stay as you are."

The play continued.

People used to say that Edwin owned the East Coast, Junius the West, and John Wilkes the South, but on this occasion, the applause was mostly for John. Asia overheard a Southerner in the audience. *Our Booth is like a young god,* the man said.

From the newspaper the next morning, they learned that the fires near the theater had been set by Southern rebels. Had they been in California, Junius said, the arsonists would have been strung up without a trial. He was for that. Edwin was for the Union. He told them that a few days earlier, he'd voted for the first time. He'd voted for Lincoln's reelection. John dissolved in rage. Edwin would see Lincoln become a king, John shouted, and have no one to blame but himself. Their mother intervened. No more talk of politics.

The next night the Winter Garden Theater saw the debut of *Hamlet* with Edwin in the title role. The play ran for two weeks, three, eight, ten, until Edwin felt the exhaustion of playing the same part, night after night. He begged for a change, but the play was still selling out. This run, which would last one hundred nights, was the making of Edwin's name. Ever after, he would be America's Hamlet. It was more than a calling, almost a cult. Edwin referred to this as "my terrible success."

It was a shame Shakespeare couldn't see him, the critics wrote, he was so exactly what Hamlet ought to be, so exactly what Shakespeare had envisioned. One morning his little daughter, Edwina, was offered an omelet. "That's my daddy," she said.

There came a night when, deadened from the long run, Edwin began to miss his cues. He had the curtain brought down, retired to his dressing room to gather himself. "O God! O God!" he said to himself. "How weary, stale, flat, and unprofitable/ Seem to me all the uses of this world."

When the ghost appeared, Edwin was not surprised. He'd been born with a caul, which meant protection, but also the ability to see spirits. Almost a year earlier, his beloved young wife had died of tuberculosis. She'd been in Boston, he in New York. He was Hamlet then, too, a week's worth of performances and often drunk when onstage. "Fatigued," one of the critics said, but others were not so kind.

The night she died, he'd felt her kiss him. "I am half frozen," she'd said. He'd stopped drinking and begun to spend his money on séances instead.

Initially he'd gotten good value; his wife sent many messages of love and encouragement. Her words were general, though, impersonal, and lately he'd been having doubts. He'd begun to host séances himself, with no professional medium in attendance. A friend described one such evening. He was seized, this friend said, by a powerful electricity and his hands began to shake faster and harder than mortal man could move. He was given pen and paper, which he soon covered in ink. But when he came back to his senses, he'd written no words, only scrawl. It had all been Edwin, he decided then, doing what Edwin did best. Night after night on the stage, Edwin made people believe.

The ghost visiting Edwin now was about the height of a tall woman or else a short man. It wore a helmet, but unlike the ghost in Hamlet, its visor was lowered so its face could not be seen. Its armor was torn and insubstantial, half chain mail, half cobweb. It stood wrapped in a blue-green light, shaking its arms. There was an icy wind. A sound like the dragging of chains. Edwin knew who it was. His father's acting had always been the full-throated sort.

"Why are you here?" Edwin asked.

"Why are you here?" his father's ghost asked back. His tone reverberated with ghostly disappointment. It was a tone Edwin knew well. "You have an audience in their seats. The papers will put it down to drink." More arm shaking, more dragging of chains.

Edwin pulled himself together and returned to the stage.

Two:

The serpent that did sting thy father's life
Now wears his crown.

Drink and the theater ran heavy in Edwin's blood. His father, Junius Brutus Booth, was famous for both. Born in England, Junius had come to America in 1821 on a ship named *The Two Brothers*. He brought with him his mistress and child. He left a wife and child behind.

Junius Brutus Booth leased a property in northern Baltimore, a remote acreage of farmland and forest. When he wasn't touring, he and his family lived in isolation in a small cabin. He refused to own slaves, forbid his family to eat meat or fish, or to kill any animal. When he inadvertently injured a copperhead with the plow, he brought it home, kept it on the hearth in a box padded with a blanket until it recovered.

Edwin's earliest memory was of returning to the farm after dark on the back of a horse. As they passed through the forest toward home, his night terror grew. There were branches that grabbed for him, the screaming of owls. The horses came to a halt. His father dismounted, swung Edwin down and across the fence. "Your foot is on your native heath, boy," his father said, and Edwin never forgot the overwhelming sense of belonging, of safety, of home that washed through him.

He was not his father's favorite child nor his mother's, either. The favorite was Henry, until he died, and then it was John Wilkes. Four of the Booth children passed before adulthood. They were all older than Edwin or would have been had they lived. These deaths drove their father into an intermittent raving madness. In later years, Junius Booth was much admired for his King Lear.

Surviving from the older set were Rosalie and Junius Jr. Edwin was the eldest of the younger set, followed by Asia, John Wilkes, and Joseph. The youngest three in particular were very close.

All but Edwin were well educated. At the age of thirteen, Edwin had been taken permanently out of school to go on the road with his father. His job was to see that Junius showed up for performances and to keep him out of taverns. It was a job no one could do with complete success. The most difficult time was after the curtain.

This seems to have been the rule: that Junius would not drink if

Edwin was watching. Some nights Edwin managed to lock his father in his room. On one of these occasions, Junius bribed the innkeeper and drank mint juleps with a straw through the keyhole.

More often Junius would insist on going out, Edwin trailing silently, close enough to watch his father, but far enough behind to escape invective. He was a child with enormous beauty and dark, anxious eyes.

His father's goal on these evenings was to give him the slip. Then Edwin would be forced to search through a midnight landscape of deserted streets for the one tavern his father was in. He received little affection and no gratitude for this. When found, Junius would curse at Edwin, shout, threaten to see him shanghaied into the navy if he didn't go away.

One afternoon his father woke up from a nap and refused to go to the theater. He was scheduled to play Richard III. "You do it," he told Edwin. "I'm sick of it."

Lacking an alternative, the manager sent Edwin onstage in his father's hump, his father's outsized costume. No warning had been given the audience, whose applause fell away into a puzzled silence. Edwin began tentatively. He tried to imitate his father's inflections, his gestures. The actors nearest him provided every possible support while those offstage crowded the wings, watching in friendly, nervous sympathy. The audience, too, found themselves filled with pity for the young boy, so obviously out of his depth, drowning in his own sleeves. He had them on the edge of their seats, wondering if he'd get through his next line, his next scene. The play ended with Edwin's first ovation. He had won it merely by surviving.

Junius Jr., Edwin's oldest brother, relocated to San Francisco, where he ran a theater company. In 1852, he talked his father into coming west on tour. No one imagined Junius Sr. could make the trip alone. Junius Jr. traveled east to pick his father up. Edwin, now eighteen years old, was to be, at long last, left at home.

The party had tickets on a steamer leaving from New York and traveling around the cape. As soon as he arrived in the city, Junius the elder and an actor friend, George Spear, shook Junius the younger loose and went off on a toot. The boat sailed without them. Clearly Junius Jr. was not up to the task. While they waited for the next boat, Edwin was fetched from Baltimore.

After the long voyage, the Booths landed finally in San Francisco. They did several engagements at Junius Jr.'s theater. Both sons took minor supporting roles, and they all made money, but lost it again in Sacramento, where the playhouses were empty. Junius the elder went home, tired and discouraged, after only two months. Edwin remained in California with Junius the younger.

Edwin turned nineteen, and celebrated his freedom from responsibility by, in his own words, drinking and whoring, often in the very taverns his father had frequented, until his older brother had had enough. Edwin then joined a company touring the mining camps. He played in Nevada City, Yuba City, Grass Valley. In Downieville, the company was caught in a tremendous blizzard. They made their slow way back over snowy roads to Nevada City.

It was night. Edwin was wandering drunk and alone along the main street in the bright moonlit snow when he saw his father coming toward him. He wore no costume, but was dressed as himself in a stained coat and shabby hat. Edwin stopped to wait for him. "Cut off even in the blossoms of my sin," his father said. A bobbing lantern shone through his body. "I'm sick to the heart of it. You do it now." The light grew brighter as his father dimmed until he finally vanished completely. The man holding the lantern was George Spear. "I've come to fetch you, boy," said George.

A letter following behind them had finally caught up. On the last leg of his voyage back, Junius Brutus Booth had drunk a glass of water from the Mississippi River that made him so ill he died within days. He'd never reached home, and his final hours had been filled with torment. In spite of the raving and drunkenness, the Booth children had adored their father. Edwin believed Junius had secretly come to watch on that night he'd stood in as Richard III, although there was no evidence to support this. Edwin believed he'd caused his father's death by choosing not to see him safely home.

He'd promised his father to someday play Hamlet. On April 25, 1853, he talked Junius Jr. into giving him the role for the first time. Junius found him inadequate and wouldn't let him repeat it. But a young critic, Ferdinand Cartwright Ewer, thought otherwise. Ewer left the San Francisco theater in great excitement and went to the newspaper offices to write a long review. Edwin Booth, he wrote, had made Hamlet "the easy, undulating, flexible thing" Shakespeare intended.

Tastes were changing. Edwin's Hamlet, as it developed over the years, was subtle where his father had been theatrical and natural where his father had declaimed. Junius Jr. may not have liked it, but Ferdinand Cartwright Ewer wrote, in that very first review of Edwin's very first Hamlet, that, in concept if not in polish, Edwin had already surpassed his father.

Three:

O horrible, O horrible, most horrible!

In February of 1865, Junius Jr. traveled to Washington, D.C. to see John Wilkes. Junius had always admired his younger brother, but now found him hysterical and unhinged on the subject of the Richmond campaign.

Their mother wrote to John that she was miserable and lonely visiting Edwin in his Boston house. "I always gave you praise," she wrote, "for being the fondest of all my boys, but since you leave me to grief I must doubt it. I am no Roman mother. I love my dear ones before country or anything else." She went back to her home in New York, where she lived with Rosalie, her oldest daughter.

In March, John Wilkes attended Lincoln's second inauguration, standing on the platform, close to the president. After that, he came to Boston briefly, charmed his little niece Edwina with stories of his childhood. These stories were remarkable in part for how little a role her father, Edwin, had in them. Edwin and John had lived completely different lives.

Then John quarreled again with Edwin about the war, and again he left the house in anger. Back in Washington he joined thousands of others on the White House lawn when Lincoln spoke from the balcony about extending voting rights to the Negroes. John retired to a bar to drink his way through his fury. A quart of brandy in, another drinker told him he'd never be the actor his father was.

"I'll be the most famous man in America," John Wilkes answered.

On the night of April 14, 1865, Edwin Booth was in Boston, playing the villain in a melodrama called *The Iron Chest* to a sold-out house. The Civil War had just ended; the city was celebrating. Edwin Booth was thirty-one years old and engaged to be married again.

Some of his audience, on the way home from the theater, heard that the president had been shot, and some of those dismissed this as idle rumor. Edwin knew nothing until the newspaper arrived the next morning. When he saw his brother's name in print, Edwin wrote later to a friend, he felt he'd been struck on the head with a hammer. Soon a message arrived from the manager of the Boston Theater. Although he prayed, the note said, that what everyone was saying about Wilkes would yet prove untrue, he thought it best and right to cancel all further performances.

Edwin's daughter, Edwina, was visiting her aunt Asia in Philadelphia. Asia read the news in the paper and collapsed. While her husband was trying to calm her, a U.S. marshal arrived, forbid them to leave the house, and put a guard at every door.

Junius Jr. was on tour in Cincinnati. When he entered his hotel lobby for breakfast, the clerk immediately sent him back upstairs. Moments later, a mob of some five hundred people arrived. They had stripped the lampposts of Junius' playbills and come to hang him. His life was saved by the hotel clerk, who convinced the mob that Junius had gone in the night, and the staff, who hid him in an attic room until the danger passed.

Mrs. Booth and Rosalie were at home in New York. A letter from John arrived that afternoon, written the day before. "I only drop you these few lines to let you know I am well." It was signed, "I am your affectionate son." His mother wrote to Edwin that her dearest hope now was that John would shoot himself. "Please don't let him live to be hanged," she wrote.

Junius Jr. was arrested, charged with conspiracy, taken to Washington and imprisoned there. A letter had been found from him to John that referenced the "oil business," the phrase so oblique it was obviously code. Asia's husband, John Sleeper Clarke, was also imprisoned. There was an irony in this: Clarke was a comic actor of great ambition. John Wilkes had warned Asia before she married him that Clarke didn't love her. All he'd wanted was the magic of the Booth name, John had said.

In Clarke's case there wasn't even a vague, incriminating phrase, only the partiality of his wife to her little brother. Asia would surely have been imprisoned herself, if she hadn't been pregnant. Instead she was put under house arrest.

It's not clear how Edwin escaped the conspiracy charges. He'd once saved Lincoln's son from a train accident. He was known as a Union man. He had powerful friends who exerted themselves. He'd been born with a caul. Somehow he stayed out of jail. Still, he couldn't leave his house; the streets were too dangerous. His daughter returned from her aunt's under police escort. His fiancée broke off their engagement by letter.

More letters arrived, hundreds of them, to all members of the Booth family. They came for months; they came for years. "I am carrying a bullet for you." "Your life is forfeit." "We hate the very name Booth." "Your next performance will be a tragedy."

John Wilkes was exposed as a debaucher as well as a murderer. Junius Sr.'s bigamy was suddenly remembered; the whole Booth clan was bastard-born. Plus there was Jewish blood. What a Shylock Junius Brutus Booth had once played! Asia's husband was furious to be in jail while Edwin was out. They were a nest of vipers, he told the press, a family of Iagos. His honor demanded he divorce his pregnant wife as soon as he regained his freedom.

Before dawn on April 26, John Wilkes Booth was discovered in a barn in the Maryland swamps. A torch was thrown inside. The straw caught immediately, illuminating the scene as clearly as if he were onstage. "I saw him standing upright," one Colonel Conger said later, "leaning on a crutch. He looked so like his brother Edwin I believed for a moment the whole pursuit to have been a mistake."

Four:

If it be now, 'tis not to come; if it be not to come, it will be now . . .

In the months that followed, Edwin could only leave the house at night. He walked for miles through the dark Boston streets, his hat pulled over his face. During the day, he hid in his house, writing letters of his own. He'd worked so hard to make the name of Booth respectable, he wrote. He repeated often the story of how he had once saved the life of Robert Lincoln on a train. At a friend's suggestion, to distract himself, he wrote an autobiography of his early childhood for his daughter to read, but then destroyed it before she could. He made several unsuccessful efforts, on his mother's behalf, to recover his brother's body. "I had such beautiful plans for the future," he said. "All is ruin and ever will be."

He was forced to Washington during the trial of the co-conspirators. The defense had planned to call him to attest to John Wilkes' insanity, and also to the charismatic power he held over the minds of others. The lawyers interviewed Edwin for several hours and then decided not to put him on the stand. While he was in the capital, he visited his brother and brother-in-law, still in jail. His brother-in-law repeated his plan to divorce Asia. He wondered aloud at Edwin's freedom.

"Those who have passed through such an ordeal," Asia wrote, "if there are any such ... never relearn to trust in human nature, they never resume their old place in the world, and they forget only in death."

Edwin thought he might go mad. He had a chronic piercing headache, frequent nightmares. His friends worried that he'd return to drink, and Tom Aldritch, one of the closest, moved into the house to keep him company. Edwin swore that he would never act again. It would be grotesque for any Booth to perform anywhere. The rest must be silence.

Nine months passed. Lewis Paine, George Atzerodt, David Herold, and Mary Surratt were hanged as co-conspirators in the prison yard before a large, enthusiastic crowd. Junius Booth and John Sleeper Clarke were released. Though he never forgave her, Asia's husband did not ask for a divorce. Instead they retreated to England, where they lived for the rest of their lives. Edwin's continued requests for his brother's body continued to go unanswered. Within a very few months, the entire Booth family, none of whom were working, was deeply in debt.

The bills mounted. The creditors pressed. "I don't know what will become of us," his mother wrote to Edwin. "I don't see how we'll survive." His mother, like his father, did not believe in subtlety.

In January, 1866, the Winter Garden Theater in New York announced Edwin's return to the stage. "Will it be *Julius Caesar*?" an outraged newspaper asked. "Will he perhaps, as would be fitting, play the assassin?"

He would be playing Hamlet.

Long before the performance, every ticket had sold. There would be such a crush as the Winter Garden had never seen before.

On the night of the performance, some without tickets forced their way in as far as the lobby. The play began. From his dressing room, Edwin Booth knew when the ghost had made his entrance. Marcellus: *Peace, break thee off; look, where it comes again.* And then Bernardo: *In the same figure, like the king that's dead.* Edwin couldn't actually hear the words. He recognized the lines from their stress and inflections. He knew the moment of them. He knew exactly how much time remained until he took his place for the second scene.

Edwin leaned into the mirror to stare past his own painted face into the space behind him. On the wall to the right of the small dressing-table mirror was a coat rack, so overwhelmed with hats and capes that it loomed over the room, casting the shadow of a very large man. Swords of all sorts lay on the table tops, boots on the floor, doublets and waistbands on the chairs.

A knock at the door. His father's old friend, George Spear, had come to beg Edwin to reconsider. What is out there, he said, what is waiting for you is not an audience so much as a mob. Yet Edwin couldn't hear them at all. It seemed they sat in a complete, uncanny silence.

"I am carrying a bullet for you." "Your life is forfeit."

No one in his family had dared to come. His daughter, Edwina, was at his mother's house. He imagined her descending the stairs in her nightgown to give her grandmother a kiss. He imagined her ascending again. He imagined her safe in her bed. He was called to take his place onstage for the second scene, but could not make his legs move.

"We hate the very name Booth." "Your next performance will be a tragedy."

Now he could hear the audience, stamping their feet, impatient at the delay. He waited for his father's ghost to arrive, ask why he kept an audience waiting in their seats. But there was only the stage manager, knocking a second time, calling with some agitation. "Mr. Booth? Mr. Booth?" What did it mean that his father had not come?

"I'm ready," Edwin said, and having said so, he could rise. He left the dressing room and took his place on the stage. The actors around him were stiff with tension.

One of the hallmarks of Edwin's Hamlet was that he made no entrance. As the curtain opened on the second scene, it often took the audience time to locate him among the busy Danish court. He sat unobtrusively off to one side, under the standard of the great Raven of Denmark, his head bowed. "Among a gaudy court," a critic had written of an earlier performance, "'he alone with them, alone,' easily prince, and nullifying their effect by the intensity and color of his gloom." On this particular night he seemed a frail figure, slight and dark and unremarkable save for the intensity and color of his gloom. The audience found him in his chair. There sat their American Hamlet.

Someone began to clap and then someone else. The audience came to their feet. The next day's review in *The Spirit of the Times* reported nine cheers, then six, then three, then nine more. The play could not continue, and as they clapped, many of them, men and women both, began to weep.

Edwin stood and came forward into the footlights. He bowed very low, and then he couldn't straighten, but continued to sink. Someone caught him from behind, just before he fell. "There, boy," his father said, unseen, a whisper in Edwin's ear as he was lifted to his feet.

When he stood again upright, the audience saw that Edwin, too, was weeping. It made them cheer him again. And again.

His fellow actors gathered tightly in, clapping their hands. His father's arms were wrapped around him. Edwin smelled his father's pipe and beyond it, the forest, the fireplace of his childhood home. "There, boy. There, boy," his father said. "Your foot is on your native heath."

The Last Worders

Charlotta was asleep in the dining car when the train arrived in San Margais. It was tempting to just leave her behind, and I tried to tell myself this wasn't a mean thought, but came to me because I, myself, might want to be left like that, just for the adventure of it. I might want to wake up hours later and miles away, bewildered and alone. I am always on the lookout for those parts of my life that could be the first scene in a movie. Of course, you could start a movie anywhere, but you wouldn't; that's my point. And so this impulse had nothing to do with the way Charlotta had begun to get on my last nerve. That's my other point. If I thought being ditched would be sort of exciting, then so did Charlotta. We felt the same about everything.

"Charlotta," I said. "Charlotta. We're here." I was on my feet, grabbing my backpack, when the train actually stopped. This threw me into the arms of a boy of about fourteen, wearing a T-shirt from the Three Mountains Soccer Camp. It was nice of him to catch me. I probably wouldn't have done that when I was fourteen. What's one tourist more or less? I tried to say some of this to Charlotta when we were on the platform and the train was already puffing fainter and fainter in the distance, winding its way like a great worm up into the Rambles Mountains. The boy hadn't gotten off with us.

It was raining, and we tented our heads with our jackets. "He was probably picking your pocket," Charlotta said. "Do you still have your wallet?" Which made me feel I'd been a fool, but when I put my hand in to check, I found, instead of taking something out, he'd put something in. I pulled out an orange piece of paper folded like a fan. When opened, flattened, it was a flier in four languages—German, Japanese, French, and English. *Open mike*, the English part said. And then, *Come to the Last Word Café. 100 Ruta de los Esclavos by the river. First drink free. Poetry Slam. To the death.*

The rain erased the words even as we read them.

"No city listed," Charlotta noted. She had taken the paper from me to look more closely. Now it was blank and limp. She refolded it, carefully so it wouldn't tear, put it in the back pocket of her pants. "Anyway, can't be here."

The town of San Margais hangs on the edge of a deep chasm. There'd been a river once. We had a geological witness. We had the historical records. But there was no river now.

"And no date for the slam," Charlotta added. "And we don't think fast on our feet. And death. That's not very appealing."

If she'd made only one objection, then she'd no interest. Ditto if she'd made two. But three was defensive; four was obsessive. Four meant that if Charlotta could ever find the Last Word Café, she was definitely going. Just because I'd been invited and she hadn't. Try to keep her out! I know this is what she felt because it's what I would have felt.

We took a room in a private house on the edge of the gorge. We had planned to lodge in the city center, more convenient to everything, but we were tired and wanted to get in out of the rain. The guidebook said this place was cheap and clean.

It was ten-thirty in the morning and the proprietress was still in her nightgown. She was a woman of about fifty, and the loss of her two front teeth had left a small dip in her upper lip. Her nightgown was imprinted with angels wearing choir robes and haloes on sticks like balloons. She spoke little English; there was a lot of pointing, most of it upward. Then we had to follow her angel butt up three flights of ladders, hauling our heavy packs. The room was large and had its own sink. There were glass doors opening onto a balcony, rain sheeting down. If you looked out, there was nothing to see. Steep nothing. Gray nothing. The dizzying null of the gorge. "You can have the bed by the doors," Charlotta offered. She was already moved in, toweling her hair.

"You," I said. I was nobody's fool.

Charlotta sang. "It is scary, in my aerie."

"Poetry?" the proprietress asked. Her dimpled lip curled slightly. She didn't have to speak the language to know bad poetry when she heard it, that lip said.

"Yes," Charlotta said. "Yes. The Last Word Café? Is where?"

"No," she answered. Maybe she'd misunderstood us. Maybe we'd misunderstood her.

A few facts about the gorge:

The gorge is very deep and very narrow. A thousand years ago a staircase was cut into the interior of the cliff. According to our guide-book, there are 839 stone steps, all worn smooth by traffic. Back when the stairs were made, there was still a river. Slaves carried water from the river up the stairs to the town. They did this all day long, down with an empty clay pitcher, up with a full one, and then different slaves carried water all during the night. The slave owners were noted for their poetry and their cleanliness. They wrote formal erotic poems about how dirty their slaves were.

One day there was an uprising. The slaves on the stairs knew nothing about it. They had their pitchers. They had the long way down and the longer way up. Slaves from the town, ex-slaves now, stood at the top and told each one as he (or she) arrived, that he (or she) was free. Some of the slaves poured their water out onto the stone steps to prove this to themselves. Some emptied their pitchers into the cistern as usual, thinking to have a nice bath later. Later all the pitchers were given to the former slave owners who now were slaves and had to carry water up from the river all day or all night.

Still later there was resentment between the town slaves, who had taken all the risks and made all the plans, and the stair slaves, who were handed their freedom. The least grateful of the latter were sent back to the stairs.

Two or three hundred years after the uprising, there was no more water. Over many generations the slaves had finally emptied the river. To honor their long labors, in memory of a job well done, slavery was abolished in San Margais. There is a holiday to commemorate this every year on May 21. May 21 is also our birthday, mine and Charlotta's. Let's not make too much of that.

Among the many factions in San Margais was one that felt there was nothing to celebrate in having once had a river and now not having one. Many bitter poems have been written on this subject, all entitled "May 21."

The shower in our pensione was excellent, the water hot and hard. Charlotta reported this to me. Since I got my choice of bed, she got the first shower. We'd been making these sorts of calculations all our lives; it kept us in balance. As long as everyone played. We were not in San Margais for the poetry.

Five years before, while we were still in high school, Charlotta and I had fallen in love with the same boy. His name was Raphael Kaplinsky. He had an accent, South African, and a motorcycle, American. "I saw him first," Charlotta said, which was true—he was in her second period World Lit class. I hadn't seen him until fifth period Chemistry.

I spoke to him first, though. "Is it supposed to be this color?" I'd asked when we were testing for acids.

"He spoke to me first," Charlotta said, which was also true since he'd answered my acid question with a shrug. And then, several days later, said "Nice boots!" to Charlotta when she came to school in calf-high red Steve Maddens.

My red Steve Maddens.

We quarreled about Raphael for weeks without settling anything. We didn't speak to each other for days at a time. All the while Raphael dated other girls. Loose and easy Deirdre. Bookish Kathy. Spiritual, ethereal Nina. Junco, the Japanese foreign-exchange student.

Eventually Charlotta and I agreed that we would both give Raphael up. Charlotta made the offer, but I'd been planning the same; I matched it instantly. There was simply no other way. We met in the yard to formalize the agreement with a ceremony. Each of us wrote the words Ms. Raphael Weldon-Kaplinsky onto a piece of paper. Then we simultaneously tore our papers into twelve little bits. We threw the bits into the fishpond and watched the carp eat them.

I knew that Charlotta would honor our agreement. I knew this because I intended to do so.

When we were little, when we were just learning to talk, Mother says Charlotta and I had a secret language. She could watch us, towheaded two-year-olds, talking to each other, and she could tell that we knew what we were saying, even if she didn't. Sometimes after telling each other a long story, we would cry. One of us would start and the other would sit struggling for a moment, lip trembling, and eventually we would both be in tears. There was a graduate student in psychology interested in studying this, but we learned English and stopped speaking our secret language before he could get his grant money together.

Mother favors Charlotta. I'm not the only one to think so; Charlotta sees it, too. Mother has learned that it's simply not possible to treat two people with equal love. She would argue that she favors us both—sometimes Charlotta, sometimes me. She would say it all equals out in the end. Maybe she's right. It isn't equal yet, but it probably hasn't ended.

Some facts from our guidebook about the San Margais Civil War. 1932–37: The underlying issues were aesthetic and economic. The trigger was an assassination.

In the middle ages, San Margais was a city-state ruled by a hereditary clergy. Even after annexation, the clergy played the dominant political role. Fra Nando came to power in the 1920s during an important poetic revival known as the Margais Movement. Its premiere voice was the great epistemological poet, Gigo. Fra Nando believed in the lessons of history. Gigo believed in the natural cadence of the street, the impenetrable nature of truth. From Day One these two were headed for a showdown.

Still, for a few years, all was politeness. Gigo received many grants and honors from the Nando regime. She was given a commission to write a poem celebrating Fra Nando's seventieth birthday. "Yes, I remember," Gigo's poem begins (in translation), "the great cloud of dragonflies grazing the lake ..." If Fra Nando's name appeared only in the dedication, at least this was accessible stuff. Nostalgic, even elegiac.

Gigo was never nostalgic. Gigo was never elegiac. To be so now expressed only her deep contempt for Fra Nando, but it was all so very rhythmical; he was completely taken in. Fra Nando set the first two lines in stone over the entrance to the city-state library and invited Gigo to be his special guest at the unveiling.

"The nature of the word is not the nature of the stone," Gigo said at the ceremony when it was her turn to speak. This was also accessible. Fra Nando went red in the face as if he'd been slapped, one hand to each cheek.

A cartel of businessmen, angry over the graduated tariff system Nando had instituted, saw the opportunity to assassinate him and have the poets blamed. Gigo was killed at a reading the same night Fra Nando was laid in state in the Catedral Nacionales. Her last words were "blind hill, grave glass," which is all anyone could have hoped. Unless she said "grave grass," and one of her acolytes changed her words in the reporting as her detractors have alleged. Anyone could think up grave grass, especially if they were dying at the time.

All that remains for certain of Gigo's work are the contemptuous two lines in stone. The Margais Movement was outlawed, its poems systematically searched out and destroyed. Attempts were made to memorize the greatest of Gigo's verses, but these had been written so as to defy memorization. A phrase here and there, much contested, survives. Nothing that suggests genius. All the books by or about the Margais Movement were burned. All the poets were imprisoned and tortured until they couldn't remember their own names, much less their own words.

There is a narrow bridge across the gorge that Charlotta can see from the doors by her bed. During the civil war, people were thrown from the bridge. There is still a handful of old men and old women here who will tell you they remember seeing that.

Raphael Kaplinsky went to our high school for only one year. We told ourselves it was good we hadn't destroyed our relationship for so short a reward. We dated other boys, boys neither of us liked. The flaws in our reasoning began to come clear.

1) Raphael Kaplinsky was ardent and oracular. You didn't meet a boy like Raphael Kaplinsky in every world lit, every chemistry class you took. He was the very first person to use the word *later* to end a conversation. Using the word *later* in this particular way was a promise. It was nothing less than messianic.

2) What if we did, someday, meet a boy we liked as much as Raphael? We were both bound to like him exactly the same. We hadn't solved our problem so much as delayed it. We were doomed to a lifetime of each-otherness unless we came up with a different plan.

We hired an internet detective to find Raphael, and he uncovered a recent credit-card trail. We had followed this trail all the way to last Sunday in San Margais. We had come to San Margais to make Raphael choose between us.

It was raining too hard to go out, plus we'd spent the night sitting up on the train. We hadn't been able to sit together, and had had a drunk on one side (Charlotta's) and a shoebox of mice on the other (mine). The mice were headed to the Snake Pit at the State Zoo. There was no way to sleep while their little paws scrabbled desperately, fruitlessly, against the cardboard. I had an impulse to set them free, but it seemed unfair to the snakes. How often in this world we are unwillingly forced to take sides! Team Mouse or Team Snake? Team Fly or Team Spider?

Charlotta and I napped during the afternoon while the glass rattled in the door frames and the rain fell. I woke up when I was too hungry to sleep. "I have got to have something to eat," Charlotta said.

—m—

The cuisine of San Margais is nothing to write home about. Charlotta and I each bought an umbrella from a street peddler and ate in a small, dark pizzeria. It was not only wet outside, but cold. The pizzeria had a large oven, which made the room pleasant to linger in, even though there was a group of Italian tourists smoking across the way.

Charlotta and I had a policy never to order the same thing off a menu. This was hard, because the same thing always sounded good to both of us, but it doubled our chances of making the right choice. Charlotta ordered a pizza called El Diablo, which was all theater and annoyed me, as we don't like hot foods. El Diablo brought tears to her eyes, and she only ate one piece, picking the olives off the rest and then helping herself to several slices of mine.

She wiped her face with a napkin, which left a rakish streak of pizza sauce on her cheek. I was irritated enough to say nothing about this. One of the Italians made his way to our table. "So," he said with no preliminaries. "American, yes? I can kiss you?"

We were nothing if not patriots. Charlotta stood at once, moved into his arms, and I saw his tongue go into her mouth. They kissed for several seconds, then Charlotta pushed him away, and now the pizza sauce was on him.

"So," she said. "Now. We need directions to the closest internet café."

The Italian drew a map on her place mat. He drew well; his map had depth and perspective. The internet café appeared to be around many corners and up many flights of stairs. The Italian decorated his map with hopeful little hearts. Charlotta took it away from him or there surely would have been more of these.

The San Margais miracle, an anecdotal account:

About ten years ago, a little boy named Bastien Brunelle was crossing the central plaza when he noticed something strange on the face of the statue of Fra Nando. He looked more closely. Fra Nando was crying large milky tears. Bastien ran home to tell his parents.

The night before, Bastien's father had had a dream. In his dream he was old and crippled, twisted up like a licorice stick. In his dream he had a dream that told him to go and bathe in the river. He woke from the dream dream and made his slow, painful way down the 839 steps. At the bottom of the gorge he waited. He heard a noise in the distance, cars on a freeway. The river arrived like a train and stopped to let him in. Bastien's father woke up and was thirty-two again, which was his proper age.

When he heard about the statue, Bastien's father remembered the dream. He followed Bastien out to the square where a crowd was gathering, growing. "Fra Nando is crying for the river," Bastien's father told the crowd. "It's a sign to us. We have to put the river back."

Bastien's father had never been a community leader. He ran a small civil war museum for tourists, filled with faked Gigo poems, and rarely bought a round for the house when he went out drinking. But now he had all the conviction of the man who sees clearly amidst the men who are confused. He organized a brigade to carry water down the steps to the bottom of the gorge and his purpose was so absolute, so inspired were his words, that people volunteered their spare hours, their children's spare hours. They signed up for slots in his schedule and carried water down the stairs for almost a week before they all lost interest and remembered Bastien's father was not the mouth of God, but a tight-assed cheat.

By this time news of the crying statue had gone out on the internet. Scientists had performed examinations. "Fakery cannot be ruled out," one said, which transformed into the headline, "No Sign of Fakery." Pilgrims began to arrive from wealthy European countries, mostly college kids with buckets, thermoses, used Starbucks cups.

They would stay two or three days, two or three weeks, hauling water down, having visions on the stairs and sex.

And then that ended, too. Every time has its task. Ours is to digitize the world's libraries. This is a big job that will take generations to complete, like the pyramids. No time for filling gorges with water. "Live lightly on the earth," the pilgrims remembered. "Leave no footprint behind." And they all went home again, or at least they left San Margais.

On odd days of the week our people-finder detective emailed Charlotta and copied me. On even, the opposite. Two days earlier Raphael had bought a hat and four postcards. He had dinner at a pricey restaurante and got a fifty-dollar cash advance. That was Charlotta's email.

Mine said that this very night, he was buying fifteen beers at the Last Word Café, San Margais.

We googled that name to a single entry. *100 Ruta de los Esclavos by the river*, it said. *Open mike. Underground music and poetry nightly.*

There were other Americans using the computers. I walked through, asking if any of them knew how to get to the Last Word Café. To Ruta de los Esclavos? They were paying by the minute. Most of them didn't look up. Those that did shook their heads.

Charlotta and I opened our umbrellas and went back out into the rain. We asked directions from everyone we saw, but very few people were on the street. They didn't know English or they disliked being accosted by tourists or they didn't like the look of our face. They hurried by without speaking. Only a single woman stopped. She took my chin in her hand to make sure she had my full attention. Her eyes were tinged in yellow, and she smelled like Irish Spring soap. "No," she said firmly. "*Me entiendes?* No for you."

We walked along the gorge, because this was the closest thing San

Margais had to a river. On one side of us, the town. The big yellow
I of Tourist Information (closed indefinitely), shops of ceramics and
cheeses, postcards, law offices, podiatrists, pubs, our own pensione.
On the other the cliff face, the air. We crossed the narrow bridge and
when we came to the 839 steps we started down them just because they
were mostly inside the cliff and therefore covered and therefore dry.
I was the one to point these things out to Charlotta. I was the one to
say we should go down.

The steps were smooth and slippery. Each one had a dip in the
center in just that place where a slave was most likely to put his (or
her) foot. Water dripped from the walls around us, but we were able
to close our umbrellas, leave them at the top to be picked up later. For
the first stretch there were lights overhead. Then we were in darkness,
except for an occasional turn, which brought an occasional opening to
the outside. A little light could carry us a long way.

We descended maybe 300 steps, and then, by one of the openings, we met an American coming up. In age she was somewhere in
that long, unidentifiable stretch from twenty-two to thirty-five. She
was carrying an empty bucket, plastic, the sort a child takes to the
seashore. She was breathless from the climb.

She stopped beside us, and we waited until she was able to speak.
"What the fuck," she said finally, "is the point of going down empty-
handed? What the fuck is the point of you?"

Charlotta had been asking sort of the same thing. What was the
point of going all the way down the stairs? Why had she let me talk
her into it? She talked me into going back. We turned and followed
the angry American up and out into the rain. It was only 300 steps,
but when we'd done them we were winded and exhausted. We went to
our room, crawled up our three ladders, and landed in a deep, dispir-
ited sleep.

It was still raining the next morning. We went to the city center and breakfasted in a little bakery. Just as we were finishing, our Italian walked in. "We kiss more, yes?" he asked me. He'd mistaken me for Charlotta. I stood up. I was always having to do her chores. His tongue ranged through my mouth as if he were looking for scraps. I tasted cigarettes, gum, things left in ashtrays.

"So," I said, pushing him away. "Now. We need directions to the Last Word Café."

And it turned out we'd almost gotten there last night, after all. The Last Word was the last stop along the 839 steps. It seemed as if I'd known this.

Our Italian said he'd been the night before. No one named Raphael had taken the mic; he was sure of this, but he thought there might have been a South African at the bar. Possibly this South African had bought him a drink. It was a very crowded room. No one had died. That was just—how is it we Americans say? Poem license?

"Raphael probably wanted to get the feel of the place before he spoke," Charlotta said. "That's what I'd do."

And me. That's what I'd do, too.

There was no point in going back before dark. We checked our email, but he was apparently still living on the cash advance; nothing had been added since the Last Word last night. We decided to spend the day as tourists, thinking Raphael might do the same. Because of the rain we had the outdoor sights mostly to ourselves. We saw the ruins of the old baths, long and narrow as lap pools, now with nets of morning glories twisted across them. Here and there the rain had filled them.

There was a Roman arch, a Moorish garden. When we were wetter than we could bear to be we paid the eight euros entrance to the civil war museum. English translation was extra, but we were on a budget; there are no bargains on last-minute tickets to San Margais. We told ourselves it was more in keeping with the spirit of Gigo if we didn't understand a thing.

The museum was small, two rooms only and dimly lit. We stood awhile beside the wall radiator, drying out and warming up. Even from that spot we could see most of the room we were in. There were three life-size dioramas—mannequins dressed as Gigo might have dressed, meeting with people Gigo might have met. We recognized the mannequin Fra Nando from the statue we'd seen in the city center, although this version was less friendly. His hand was on Gigo's shoulder, his expression enigmatic. She was looking past him up at something tall and transcendent. There was clothing laid out, male and female, in glass cases along with playbills, baptismal certificates, baby pictures. Stapled to the wall were a series of book illustrations—a bandito seizing a woman on a balcony. The woman shaking free, leaping to her death. A story Gigo had written? A family legend? A scene from the civil war? All of the above? The man who sold us our tickets, Señor Brunelle, was conducting a tour for an elderly British couple, but since we hadn't paid it would be wrong to stand where we could hear. We were careful not to do so.

We spoke to Señor Brunelle after. We made polite noises about the museum, so interesting, we said. So unexpected. And then Charlotta asked him what he knew about the Last Word Café.

"For tourists," he said. "Myself, my family, we don't go down the steps anymore." He was clearly sad about this. "All tourists now."

"What does it mean?" Charlotta asked first. "Poetry to the death?"

"Which word needs definition? Poetry? Or Death?"

"I know the words."

"Then I am no more help," Señor Brunelle told her.

"Why does it say it's by the river when there's no river?" Charlotta asked second.

"Always a river. In San Margais, always a river. Sometimes in your mind. Sometimes in the gorge. Either way, a river."

"Is there any reason we shouldn't go?" Charlotta asked third.

"Go. You go. You won't get in," Señor Brunelle said. He said this to Charlotta. He didn't say it to me.

The Last Worders:

On the night Raphael took the open mic at the Last Word Café, he did three poems. He spoke ten minutes. He stood on the stage and he didn't try to move; he didn't try to make it sing; he made no effort to sell his words. The light fell in a small circle on his face so that, most of the time, his eyes were closed. He was beautiful. The people listening also closed their eyes, and that made him more beautiful still. The women, the men who'd wanted him when he started to talk no longer did so. He was beyond that, unfuckable. For the rest of their lives, they'd be undone by the mere sound of his name. The ones who spoke English tried to write down some part of what he'd said on their napkins, in their travel journals. They made lists of words—childhood, ice, yes. Gleaming, yes, yesterday.

These are the facts. Anyone can figure out this much.

For the rest, you had to be there. What was heard, the things people suddenly knew, the things people suddenly felt—none of that could be said in any way that could be passed along. By the time Raphael had finished, everyone listening, everyone there for those few minutes on that night at the Last Word Café, had been set free.

These people climbed the steps afterward in absolute silence. They did not go back, not a single one of them, to their marriages, their families, their jobs, their lives. They walked to the city center and they sat in the square on the edge of the fountain at the feet of the friendly Fra Nando and they knew where they were in a way they had never known it before. They tried to talk about what to do next. Words came back to them slowly. Between them, they spoke a dozen different languages, all useless now.

You could have started the movie of any one of them there, at the feet of the stone statue. It didn't matter what they could and couldn't say; they all knew the situation. Whatever they did next would be done together. They could not imagine, ever again, being with anyone who had not been there, in the Last Word Café, on the night Raphael Kaplinsky spoke.

There were details to be ironed out. How to get the money to eat. Where to live, where to sleep. How to survive now, in a suddenly clueless world.

But there was time to make these decisions. Those who had cars fetched them. Those who did not climbed in, fastened their seat belts. On the night Raphael Kaplinsky spoke at the Last Word Café, the patrons caravanned out of town without a last word to anyone. The rest of us would not hear of the Last Worders again until one of them went on *Larry King Live* and filled a two-hour show with a two-hour silence.

Or else they all died.

Charlotta and I had dinner by ourselves in the converted basement of an old hotel. The candles flickered our shadows about so we were, on all sides, surrounded by us. Charlotta had the trout. It had been cooked dry, and was filled with small bones. Every time she put a bite in her mouth, she pulled the tiny bones out. I had the mussels. The sauce was stiff and gluey. Most of the shells hadn't opened. The food in San Margais is nothing to write home about.

We finished the meal with old apples and young wine. We were both nervous, now that it came down to it, about seeing Raphael again. Each of us secretly wondered, could we live with Raphael's choice?

However it went? Could I be happy for Charlotta, if it came to that? I asked myself. Could I bear watching her forced to be happy for me? I sipped my wine and ran through every moment of my relationship with Raphael for reassurance. That stuff about the acid experiment. How much he liked my boots. "Let's go," Charlotta said, and we were a bit unsteady from the wine, which, in retrospect, with an evening of 839 steps ahead of us, was not smart.

We crossed the bridge in a high wind. The rain came in sideways; the wind turned our umbrellas inside out. Charlotta was thrown against the rope rails and grabbed on to me. If she'd fallen, she would have taken me with her. If I saved her, I saved us both. Our umbrellas went together into the gorge.

We reached the steps and began to descend, sometimes with light, sometimes feeling our way in the darkness. About one hundred steps up from the bottom, a room had been carved out of the rock. Once slave owners had sat at their leisure there, washing and rewashing their hands and feet, overseeing the slaves on the stairs. Later the room had been closed off with the addition of a heavy metal door. A posting had been set on a sawhorse outside. The Last Word Café, the English part of it said. Not for Everyone.

The door was latched. Charlotta pounded on it with her fist until it opened. A man in a tuxedo with a wide orange cummerbund stepped out. He shook his head. "American?" he asked. "And empty-handed? That's no way to make a river."

"We're here for the poetry," Charlotta told him, and he shook his head again.

"Invitation only."

And Charlotta reached into the back pocket of her pants. Charlotta pulled out the orange paper given to me by the boy on the train. The man took it. He threw it into a small basket with many other such papers. He stood aside and let Charlotta enter.

He stepped back to block me. "Invitation only."

"That was my invitation," I told him. "Charlotta!" She looked back at me, over her shoulder, without really turning around. "Tell him. Tell him that invitation was for me. Tell him how Señor Brunelle told you you wouldn't get in."

"So?" said Charlotta. "That woman on the street told you you wouldn't get in."

But I had figured that part out. "She mistook me for you," I said.

Beyond the door I could see Raphael climbing onto the dais. I could hear the room growing silent. I could see Charlotta's back sliding into a crowd of people like a knife into water. The door swung toward my face. The latch fell.

I stayed a long time by that door, but no sounds came through. Finally I walked down the last hundred steps. I was alone at the bottom of the gorge where the rain fell and fell and there was no river. I would never have done to Charlotta what she had done to me.

It took me more than an hour to climb back up. I had to stop many, many times to rest, airless, heart throbbing, legs aching, light-headed in the dark. No one met me at the top.

The Dark

In the summer of 1954, Anna and Richard Becker disappeared from Yosemite National Park along with Paul Becker, their three-year-old son. Their campsite was intact; two paper plates with half-eaten frankfurters remained on the picnic table, and a third frankfurter was in the trash. The rangers took several black-and-white photographs of the meal, which, when blown up to eight by ten, as part of the investigation, showed clearly the words *love bites*, carved into the wooden picnic table many years ago. There appeared to be some fresh scratches as well; the expert witness at the trial attributed them, with no great assurance, to raccoon.

The Beckers' car was still backed into the campsite, a green De Soto with a spare key under the right bumper and half a tank of gas. Inside the tent, two sleeping bags had been zipped together marital style and laid on a large tarp. A smaller flannel bag was spread over an inflated pool raft. Toiletries included three toothbrushes; Ipana toothpaste, squeezed in the middle; Ivory soap; three washcloths; and one towel. The newspapers discreetly made no mention of Anna's diaphragm, which remained powdered with talc, inside its pink shell, or of the fact that Paul apparently still took a bottle to bed with him.

Their nearest neighbor had seen nothing. He had been in his hammock, he said, listening to the game. Of course, the reception in Yosemite was lousy. At home he had a shortwave set; he said he had once pulled in Dover, clear as a bell. "You had to really concentrate to hear the game," he told the rangers. "You could've dropped the bomb. I wouldn't have noticed."

Anna Becker's mother, Edna, received a postcard postmarked a day earlier. "Seen the firefall," it said simply. "Home Wednesday. Love." Edna identified the bottle. "Oh yes, that's Paul's bokkie," she told the police. She dissolved into tears. "He never goes anywhere without it," she said.

In the spring of 1960, Mark Cooper and Manuel Rodriguez went on a fishing expedition in Yosemite. They set up a base camp in Tuolumne Meadows and went off to pursue steelhead. They were gone from camp approximately six hours, leaving their food and a six-pack of beer zipped inside their backpacks zipped inside their tent. When they returned, both beer and food were gone. Canine footprints circled the tent, but a small and mysterious handprint remained on the tent flap. "Raccoon," said the rangers who hadn't seen it. The tent and packs were undamaged. Whatever had taken the food had worked the zippers. "Has to be raccoon."

The last time Manuel had gone backpacking, he'd suspended his pack from a tree to protect it. A deer had stopped to investigate, and when Manuel shouted to warn it off the deer hooked the pack over its antlers in a panic, tearing the pack loose from the branch and carrying it away. Pack and antlers were so entangled, Manuel imagined the deer must have worn his provisions and clean shirts until antler-shedding season. He reported that incident to the rangers, too, but what could anyone do? He was reminded of it, guiltily, every time he read *Thidwick the Big-Hearted Moose* to his four-year-old son.

Manuel and Mark arrived home three days early. Manuel's wife said she'd been expecting him.

She emptied his pack. "Where's the can opener?" she asked. "It's there somewhere," said Manuel. "It's not," she said. "Check the shirt pocket."

"It's not here." Manuel's wife held the pack upside down and shook it. Dead leaves fell out. "How were you going to drink the beer?" she asked.

In August of 1962, Caroline Crosby, a teenager from Palo Alto, accompanied her family on a forced march from Tuolumne Meadows to Vogelsang. She carried fourteen pounds in a pack with an aluminum frame—and her father said it was the lightest pack on the market, and she should be able to carry one-third her weight, so fourteen pounds was nothing, but her pack stabbed her continuously in one coin-sized spot just below her right shoulder, and it still hurt the next morning. Her boots left a blister on her right heel, and her pack straps had rubbed. Her father had bought her a mummy bag with no zipper so as to minimize its weight; it was stiflingly hot, and she sweated all night. She missed an overnight at Ann Watson's house, where Ann showed them her sister's Mark Eden bust developer, and her sister retaliated by freezing all their bras behind the Twin Pops. She missed *The Beverly Hillbillies.*

Caroline's father had quit smoking just for the duration of the trip, so as to spare himself the weight of cigarettes, and made continual comments about Nature, which were laudatory in content and increasingly abusive in tone. Caroline's mother kept telling her to smile.

In the morning her father mixed half a cup of stream water into a packet of powdered eggs and cooked them over a Coleman stove. "Damn fine breakfast," he told Caroline intimidatingly as she stared in horror at her plate. "Out here in God's own country. What else could you ask for?" He turned to Caroline's mother, who was still trying to

Karen Joy Fowler

get a pot of water to come to a boil. "Where's the goddamn coffee?" he asked. He went to the stream to brush his teeth with a toothbrush he had sawed the handle from in order to save the weight. Her mother told her to please make a little effort to be cheerful and not spoil the trip for everyone.

One week later she was in Letterman Hospital in San Francisco. The diagnosis was septicemic plague.

Which is finally where I come into the story. My name is Keith Harmon. BA in history with a special emphasis on epidemics. I probably know as much as anyone about the plague of Athens. Typhus. Tarantism. Tsutsugamushi fever. It's an odder historical specialty than it ought to be. More battles have been decided by disease than by generals—and if you don't believe me, take a closer look at the Crusades or the fall of the Roman Empire or Napoleon's Russian campaign.

My MA is in public administration. Vietnam veteran, too, but in 1962 I worked for the state of California as part of the plague-monitoring team. When Letterman's reported a plague victim, Sacramento sent me down to talk to her.

Caroline had been moved to a private room. "You're going to be fine," I told her. Of course, she was. We still lose people to the pneumonic plague, but the slower form is easily cured. The only tricky part is making the diagnosis.

"I don't feel well. I don't like the food," she said. She pointed out Letterman's Tuesday menu. "Hawaiian Delight. You know what that is? Green Jell-O with a canned pineapple ring on top. What's delightful about that?" She was feverish and lethargic. Her hair lay limply about her head, and she kept tangling it in her fingers as she talked. "I'm missing a lot of school." Impossible to tell if this last was a complaint or a boast. She raised her bed to a sitting position and spent

56

most of the rest of the interview looking out the window, making it clear that a view of the Letterman parking lot was more arresting than a conversation with an old man like me. She seemed younger than fifteen. Of course, everyone in a hospital bed feels young. Helpless. "Will you ask them to let me wash and set my hair?"

I pulled a chair over to the bed. "I need to know if you've been anywhere unusual recently. We know about Yosemite. Anywhere else. Hiking out around the airport, for instance." The plague is endemic in the San Bruno Mountains by the San Francisco Airport. That particular species of flea doesn't bite humans, though. Or so we'd always thought. "It's kind of a romantic spot for some teenagers, isn't it?"

I've seen some withering adolescent stares in my time, but this one was practiced. I still remember it. I may be sick, it said, but at least I'm not an idiot. "Out by the airport?" she said. "Oh, right. Real romantic. The radio playing and those 727s overhead. Give me a break."

"Let's talk about Yosemite, then."

She softened a little. "In Palo Alto we go to the water temple," she informed me. "And, no, I haven't been there, either. My parents *made* me go to Yosemite. And now I've got bubonic plague." Her tone was one of satisfaction. "I think it was the powdered eggs. They *made* me eat them. I've been sick ever since."

"Did you see any unusual wildlife there? Did you play with any squirrels?"

"Oh, right," she said. "I always play with squirrels. Birds sit on my fingers." She resumed the stare. "My parents didn't tell you what I saw?"

"No," I said.

"Figures." Caroline combed her fingers through her hair. "If I had a brush, I could at least rat it. Will you ask the doctors to bring me a brush?"

"What did you see, Caroline?"

"Nothing. According to my parents. No big deal." She looked out at the parking lot. "I saw a boy."

She wouldn't look at me, but she finished her story. I heard about the mummy bag and the overnight party she missed. I heard about the eggs. Apparently, the altercation over breakfast had escalated, culminating in Caroline's refusal to accompany her parents on a brisk hike to Ireland Lake. She stayed behind, lying on top of her sleeping bag and reading the part of *Green Mansions* where Abel eats a fine meal of anteater flesh. "After the breakfast I had, my mouth was watering," she told me. Something made her look up suddenly from her book. She said it wasn't a sound. She said it was a silence.

A naked boy dipped his hands into the stream and licked the water from his fingers. His fingernails curled toward his palms like claws. "Hey," Caroline told me she told him. She could see his penis and everything. The boy gave her a quick look and then backed away into the trees. She went back to her book.

She described him to her family when they returned. "Real dirty," she said. "Real hairy."

"You have a very superior attitude," her mother noted. "It's going to get you in trouble someday."

"Fine," said Caroline, feeling superior. "Don't believe me." She made a vow never to tell her parents anything again. "And I never will," she told me. "Not if I have to eat powdered eggs until I die."

At this time there started a plague. It appeared not in one part of the world only, not in one race of men only, and not in any particular season; but it spread over the entire earth, and afflicted all without mercy of both sexes and of every age. It began in Egypt, at Pelusium; thence it spread to Alexandria and to the rest of Egypt; then went to Palestine, and from there over the whole world. . . .

In the second year, in the spring, it reached Byzantium and began in the following manner: To many there appeared phantoms in human form. Those who were so encountered, were struck by a blow from the phantom, and so contracted the disease. Others locked themselves into their houses. But then the phantoms appeared to them in dreams, or they heard voices that told them that they had been selected for death.

This comes from Procopius's account of the first pandemic, A.D. 541, *De Bello Persico*, chapter XXII. It's the only explanation I can give you for why Caroline's story made me so uneasy, why I chose not to mention it to anyone. I thought she'd had a fever dream, but thinking this didn't settle me any. I talked to her parents briefly and then went back to Sacramento to write my report.

We have no way of calculating the deaths in the first pandemic. Gibbon says that during three months, five to ten thousand people died daily in Constantinople, and many Eastern cities were completely abandoned.

The second pandemic began in 1346. It was the darkest time the planet has known. A third of the world died. The Jews were blamed, and, throughout Europe, pogroms occurred wherever sufficient health remained for the activity. When murdering Jews provided no alleviation, a committee of doctors at the University of Paris concluded the plague was the result of an unfortunate conjunction of Saturn, Jupiter, and Mars.

The third pandemic occurred in Europe during the fifteenth to eighteenth centuries. The fourth began in China in 1855. It reached Hong Kong in 1894, where Alexandre Yersin of the Institut Pasteur at last identified the responsible bacilli. By 1898 the disease had killed six million people in India. Dr. Paul-Louis Simond, also working for the Institut Pasteur, but stationed in Bombay, finally identified fleas as the primary carriers. "On June 2, 1898, I was overwhelmed," he wrote.

Karen Joy Fowler

"I had just unveiled a secret which had tormented man for so long."

His discoveries went unnoticed for another decade or so. On June 27, 1899, the disease came to San Francisco. The governor of California, acting in protection of business interests, made it a felony to publicize the presence of the plague. People died instead of *syphilitic septicemia*. Because of this deception, thirteen of the Western states are still designated plague areas.

The state team went into the high country in early October. Think of us as soldiers. One of the great mysteries of history is why the plague finally disappeared. The rats are still here. The fleas are still here. The disease is still here; it shows up in isolated cases like Caroline's. Only the epidemic is missing. We're in the middle of the fourth assault. The enemy is elusive. The war is unwinnable. We remain vigilant.

The Vogelsang Camp had already been closed for the winter. No snow yet, but the days were chilly and the nights below freezing. If the plague was present, it wasn't really going to be a problem until spring. We amused ourselves, poking sticks into warm burrows looking for dead rodents. We set out some traps. Not many. You don't want to decrease the rodent population. Deprive the fleas of their natural hosts, and they just look for replacements. They just bring the war home.

We picked up a few bodies, but no positives. We could have dusted the place anyway as a precaution. *Silent Spring* came out in 1962, but I hadn't read it.

I saw the coyote on the fourth day. She came out of a hole on the bank of Lewis Creek and stood for a minute with her nose in the air. She was grayed with age around her muzzle, possibly a bit arthritic. She shook out one hind leg. She shook out the other. Then, right as I watched, Caroline's boy climbed out of the burrow after the coyote.

I couldn't see the boy's face. There was too much hair in the way. But his body was hairless, and even though his movements were peculiar and inhuman, I never thought that he was anything but a boy. Twelve years old or maybe thirteen, I thought, although small for thirteen. Wild as a wolf, obviously. Raised by coyotes maybe. But clearly human. Circumcised, if anyone is interested.

I didn't move. I forgot about Procopius and stepped into the *National Enquirer* instead. Marilyn was in my den. Elvis was in my rinse cycle. It was my lucky day. I was amusing myself when I should have been awed. It was a stupid mistake. I wish now that I'd been someone different.

The boy yawned and closed his eyes, then shook himself awake and followed the coyote along the creek and out of sight. I went back to camp. The next morning we surrounded the hole and netted them coming out. This is the moment it stopped being such a lark. This is an uncomfortable memory. The coyote was terrified, and we let her go. The boy was terrified, and we kept him. He scratched us and bit and snarled. He cut me, and I thought it was one of his nails, but he turned out to be holding a can opener. He was covered with fleas, fifty or sixty of them visible at a time, which jumped from him to us, and they all bit, too. It was like being attacked by a cloud. We sprayed the burrow and the boy and ourselves, but we'd all been bitten by then. We took an immediate blood sample. The boy screamed and rolled his eyes all the way through it. The reading was negative. By the time we all calmed down, the boy really didn't like us.

Clint and I tied him up, and we took turns carrying him down to Tuolumne. His odor was somewhere between dog and boy, and worse than both. We tried to clean him up in the showers at the ranger station. Clint and I both had to strip to do this, so God knows what he must have thought we were about. He reacted to the touch of water as if it burned. There was no way to shampoo his hair, and no one with the strength to cut it. So we settled for washing his face and hands, put our clothes back on, gave him a sweater that he dropped by the drain, put him in the backseat of my Rambler, and drove to Sacramento. He cried most of the way, and when we went around curves he allowed his body to be flung unresisting from one side of the car to the other, occasionally knocking his head against the door handle with a loud, painful sound.

I bought him a ham sandwich when we stopped for gas in Modesto, but he wouldn't eat it. He was a nice-looking kid, had a normal face, freckled, with blue eyes, brown hair, and if he'd had a haircut you could have imagined him in some Sears catalog modeling raincoats.

One of life's little ironies. It was October 14. We rescue a wild boy from isolation and deprivation and winter in the mountains. We bring him civilization and human contact. We bring him straight into the Cuban Missile Crisis.

Maybe that's why you don't remember reading about him in the paper. We turned him over to the state of California, which had other things on its mind.

The state put him in Mercy Hospital and assigned maybe a hundred doctors to the case. I was sent back to Yosemite to continue looking for fleas. The next time I saw the boy, about a week had passed. He'd been cleaned up, of course. Scoured of parasites, inside and out. Measured. He was just over four feet tall and weighed seventy-five pounds. His head was all but shaved so as not to interfere with the various neurological tests, which had turned out normal and were being redone. He had been observed rocking in a seated position, left to right and back to front, mouth closed, chin up, eyes staring at nothing. Occasionally he had small spasms, convulsive movements, which suggested abnormalities in the nervous system. His teeth needed extensive work. He was sleeping under his bed. He wouldn't touch his Hawaiian Delight. He liked us even less than before.

About this time I had a brief conversation with a doctor whose name I didn't notice. I was never able to find him again. Red-haired doctor with glasses. Maybe thirty, thirty-two years old. "He's got some unusual musculature," this red-haired doctor told me. "Quite singular. Especially the development of the legs. He's shown us some really surprising capabilities." The boy started to howl, an unpleasant, inhuman sound that started in his throat and ended in yours. It was so unhappy. It made me so unhappy to hear it. I never followed up on what the doctor had said.

I felt peculiar about the boy, responsible for him. He had such a *boyish* face. I visited several times, and I took him little presents, a Dodgers baseball cap and an illustrated *Goldilocks and the Three Bears* with the words printed big. Pretty silly, I suppose, but what would you have gotten? I drove to Fresno and asked Manuel Rodriguez if he could identify the can opener. "Not with any assurance," he said. I talked personally to Sergeant Redburn, the man from Missing Persons. When he told me about the Beckers, I went to the state library and read the newspaper articles for myself. Sergeant Redburn thought the boy might be just about the same age as Paul Becker, and I thought so, too. And I know the sergeant went to talk to Anna Becker's mother about it, because he told me she was going to come and try to identify the boy.

By now it's November. Suddenly I get a call sending me back to Yosemite. In Sacramento they claim the team has reported a positive, but when I arrive in Yosemite, the whole team denies it. Fleas are astounding creatures. They can be frozen for a year or more and then revived to full activity. But November in the mountains is a stupid time to be out looking for them. It's already snowed once, and it snows again, so that I can't get my team back out. We spend three weeks in the ranger station at Vogelsang huddled around our camp stoves while they air-drop supplies to us. And when I get back, a doctor I've never seen before, a Dr. Frank Li, tells me the boy, who was not Paul Becker, died suddenly of a seizure while he slept. I have to work hard to put away the sense that it was my fault, that I should have left the boy where he belonged.

And then I hear Sergeant Redburn has jumped off the Golden Gate Bridge.

Non Gratum Anus Rodentum. Not worth a rat's ass. This was the unofficial motto of the tunnel rats. We're leaping ahead here. Now it's 1967. Vietnam. Does the name Cu Chi mean anything to you? If not, why not? The district of Cu Chi is the most bombed, shelled, gassed, strafed, defoliated, and destroyed piece of earth in the history of warfare. And beneath Cu Chi runs the most complex part of a network of tunnels that connects Saigon all the way to the Cambodian border.

I want you to imagine, for a moment, a battle fought entirely in the dark. Imagine that you are in a hole that is too hot and too small. You cannot stand up; you must move on your hands and knees by touch and hearing alone through a terrain you can't see toward an enemy you can't see. At any moment you might trip a mine, put your hand on a snake, put your face on a decaying corpse. You know people who have done all three of these things. At any moment the air you breathe might turn to gas, the tunnel become so small you can't get back out; you could fall into a well of water and drown; you could be buried alive. If you are lucky, you will put your knife into an enemy you may never see before he puts his knife into you. In Cu Chi the Vietnamese and the Americans created, inch by inch, body part by body part, an entirely new type of warfare.

Among the Vietnamese who survived are soldiers who lived in the tiny underground tunnels without surfacing for five solid years. Their eyesight was permanently damaged. They suffered constant malnutrition, felt lucky when they could eat spoiled rice and rats. Self-deprivation was their weapon; they used it to force the soldiers of the most technically advanced army in the world to face them with knives, one-on-one, underground, in the dark.

On the American side, the tunnel rats were all volunteers. You can't force a man to do what he cannot do. Most Americans hyperventilated, had attacks of claustrophobia, were too big. The tunnel rats could be no bigger than the Vietnamese, or they wouldn't fit through the tunnels. Most of the tunnel rats were Puerto Ricans and other Hispanics. They stopped wearing after shave so the Vietcong wouldn't smell them. They stopped chewing gum, smoking, and eating candy because it impaired their ability to sense the enemy. They had to develop the sonar of bats. They had, in their own words, to become animals. What they did in the tunnels, they said, was unnatural.

In 1967 I was attached to the 521st Medical Detachment. I was an old man by Vietnamese standards, but then, I hadn't come to fight in the Vietnam War. Remember that the fourth pandemic began in China. Just before he died, Chinese poet Shih Tao-nan wrote:

Few days following the death of the rats,
Men pass away like falling walls.

Between 1965 and 1970, 24,848 cases of the plague were reported in Vietnam.

War is the perfect breeding ground for disease. They always go together, the trinity: war, disease, and cruelty. Disease was my war. I'd been sent to Vietnam to keep my war from interfering with everybody else's war.

Karen Joy Fowler

In March we received by special courier a package containing three dead rats. The rats had been found—already dead, but leashed—inside a tunnel in Hau Nghia province. Also found—but not sent to us—were a syringe, a phial containing yellow fluid, and several cages. I did the test myself. One of the dead rats carried the plague.

There has been speculation that the Vietcong were trying to use plague rats as weapons. It's also possible they were merely testing the rats prior to eating them themselves. In the end, it makes little difference. The plague was there in the tunnels whether the Vietcong used it or not.

I set up a tent outside Cu Chi town to give boosters to the tunnel rats. One of the men I inoculated was David Rivera. "David has been into the tunnels so many times, he's a legend," his companions told me.

"Yeah," said David. "Right. Me and Victor."

"Victor Charlie?" I said. I was just making conversation. I could see David, whatever his record in the tunnels, was afraid of the needle. He held out one stiff arm. I was trying to get him to relax.

"No. Not hardly. Victor is the one." He took his shot, put his shirt back on, gave up his place to the next man in line.

"Victor can see in the dark," the next man told me.

"Victor Charlie?" I asked again.

"No," the man said impatiently.

"You want to know about Victor?" David said. "Let me tell you about Victor. Victor's the one who comes when someone goes down and doesn't come back out."

"Victor can go faster on his hands and knees than most men can run," the other man said. I pressed cotton on his arm after I withdrew the needle; he got up from the table. A third man sat down and took off his shirt.

David still stood next to me. "I go into this tunnel. I'm not too scared, because I think it's cold; I'm not *feeling* anybody else there, and

I'm maybe a quarter of a mile in, on my hands and knees, when I can almost see a hole in front of me, blacker than anything else in the tunnel, which is all black, you know. So I go into the hole, feeling my way, and I have this funny sense like I'm not moving into the hole; the hole is moving over to me. I put out my hands, and the ground moves under them."

"Shit," said the third man. I didn't know if it was David's story or the shot. A fourth man sat down.

"I risk a light, and the whole tunnel is covered with spiders, covered like wallpaper, only worse, two or three bodies thick," David said. "I'm sitting on them, and the spiders are already inside my pants and inside my shirt and covering my arms—and it's fucking Vietnam, you know; I don't even know if they're poisonous or not. Don't care, really, because I'm going to die just from having them on me. I can feel them moving toward my face. So I start to scream, and then this little guy comes and pulls me back out a ways, and then he sits for maybe half an hour, calm as can be, picking spiders off me. When I decide to live after all, I go back out. I tell everybody. 'That was Victor,' they say. 'Had to be Victor.'"

"I know a guy says Victor pulled him from a hole," the fourth soldier said. "He falls through a false floor down maybe twelve straight feet into this tiny little trap with straight walls all around and no way up, and Victor comes down after him. *Jumps* back out, holding the guy in his arms. Twelve feet; the guy swears it."

"Tiny little guy," said David. "Even for VC, this guy'd be tiny."

"He just looks tiny," the second soldier said. "I know a guy saw Victor buried under more than a ton of dirt. Victor just digs his way out again. No broken bones, no nothing."

Inexcusably slow, and I'd been told twice, but I had just figured out that Victor wasn't short for VC. "I'd better inoculate this Victor," I said. "You think you could send him in?"

The men stared at me. "You don't get it, do you?" said David.

"Victor don't report," the fourth man says.

"No CO," says the third man.

"No unit."   ·

"He's got the uniform," the second man tells me. "So we don't know if he's special forces of some sort or if he's AWOL down in the tunnels."

"Victor lives in the tunnels," said David. "Nobody up top has ever seen him."

I tried to talk to one of the doctors about it. "Tunnel vision," he told me. "We get a lot of that. Forget it."

In May we got a report of more rats—some leashed, some in cages—in a tunnel near Ah Nhon Tay village in the Ho Bo Woods. But no one wanted to go in and get them, because these rats were alive. And somebody got the idea this was my job, and somebody else agreed. They would clear the tunnel of VC first, they promised me. So I volunteered.

Let me tell you about rats. Maybe they're not responsible for the plague, but they're still destructive to every kind of life-form and beneficial to none. They eat anything that lets them. They breed during all seasons. They kill their own kind; they can do it singly, but they can also organize and attack in hordes. The brown rat is currently embroiled in a war of extinction against the black rat. Most animals behave better than that.

I'm not afraid of rats. I read somewhere that about the turn of the century, a man in western Illinois heard a rustling in his fields one night. He got out of bed and went to the back door, and behind his house he saw a great mass of rats that stretched all the way to the horizon. I suppose this would have frightened me. All those naked tails in the moonlight. But I thought I could handle a few rats in cages, no problem.

It wasn't hard to locate them. I was on my hands and knees, but using a flashlight. I thought there might be some loose rats, too, and that I ought to look at least; and I'd also heard that there was an abandoned VC hospital in the tunnel that I was curious about. So I left the cages and poked around in the tunnels a bit; and when I'd had enough, I started back to get the rats, and I hit a water trap. There hadn't been a water trap before, so I knew I must have taken a wrong turn. I went back a bit, took another turn, and then another, and hit the water trap again. By now I was starting to panic. I couldn't find anything I'd ever seen before except the damn water. I went back again, farther without turning, took a turn, hit the trap.

I must have tried seven, eight times. I no longer thought the tunnel was cold. I thought the VC had closed the door on my original route so that I wouldn't find it again. I thought they were watching every move I made, pretty easy with me waving my flashlight about. I switched it off. I could hear them in the dark, their eyelids closing and opening, their hands tightening on their knives. I was sweating, head to toe, like I was ill, like I had the mysterious English sweating sickness or the *Suette des Picards*.

And I knew that to get back to the entrance, I had to go into the water. I sat and thought that through, and when I finished, I wasn't the same man I'd been when I began the thought.

It would have been bad to have to crawl back through the tunnels with no light. To go into the water with no light, not knowing how much water there was, not knowing if one lungful of air would be enough or if there were underwater turns so you might get lost before you found air again, was something you'd have to be crazy to do. I had to do it, so I had to be crazy first. It wasn't as hard as you might think. It took me only a minute.

Karen Joy Fowler

I filled my lungs as full as I could. Emptied them once. Filled them again and dove in. Someone grabbed me by the ankle and hauled me back out. It frightened me so much I swallowed water, so I came up coughing and kicking. The hand released me at once, and I lay there for a bit, dripping water and still sweating, too, feeling the part of the tunnel that was directly below my body turn to mud, while I tried to convince myself that no one was touching me.

Then I was crazy enough to turn my light on. Far down the tunnel, just within range of the light, knelt a little kid dressed in the uniform of the rats. I tried to get closer to him. He moved away, just the same amount I had moved, always just in the light. I followed him down one tunnel, around a turn, down another. Outside, the sun rose and set. We crawled for days. My right knee began to bleed.

"Talk to me," I asked him. He didn't.

Finally he stood up ahead of me. I could see the rat cages, and I knew where the entrance was behind him. And then he was gone. I tried to follow with my flashlight, but he'd jumped or something. He was just gone.

"Victor," Rat Six told me when I finally came out. "Goddamn Victor."

Maybe so. If Victor was the same little boy I put a net over in the high country in Yosemite.

When I came out, they told me less than three hours had passed. I didn't believe them. I told them about Victor. Most of them didn't believe me. Nobody outside the tunnels believed in Victor. "We just sent home one of the rats," a doctor told me. "He emptied his whole gun into a tunnel. Claimed there were VC all around him, but that he got them. He shot every one. Only, when we went down to clean it up, there were no bodies. All his bullets were found in the walls.

"Tunnel vision. Everyone sees things. It's the dark. Your eyes no longer impose any limit on the things you can see."

I didn't listen. I made demands right up the chain of command for records: recruitment, AWOLs, special projects. I wanted to talk to everyone who'd ever seen Victor. I wrote Clint to see what he remembered of the drive back from Yosemite. I wrote a thousand letters to Mercy Hospital, telling them I'd uncovered their little game. I demanded to speak with the red-haired doctor with glasses whose name I never knew. I wrote the Curry Company and suggested they conduct a private investigation into the supposed suicide of Sergeant Redburn. I asked the CIA what they had done with Paul's parents. That part was paranoid. I was so unstrung I thought they'd killed his parents and given him to the coyote to raise him up for the tunnel wars. When I calmed down, I knew the CIA would never be so far-sighted. I knew they'd just gotten lucky. I didn't know what happened to the parents; still don't.

There were so many crazy people in Vietnam, it could take them a long time to notice a new one, but I made a lot of noise. A team of three doctors talked to me for a total of seven hours. Then they said I was suffering from delayed guilt over the death of my little dog-boy, and that it surfaced, along with every other weak link in my personality, in the stress and the darkness of the tunnels. They sent me home. I missed the moon landing, because I was having a nice little time in a hospital of my own.

When I was finally and truly released, I went looking for Caroline Crosby. The Crosbys still lived in Palo Alto, but Caroline did not. She'd started college at Berkeley, but then she'd dropped out. Her parents hadn't seen her for several months.

Her mother took me through their beautiful house and showed me Caroline's old room. She had a canopy bed and her own bathroom. There was a mirror with old pictures of some boy on it. A throw rug with roses. There was a lot of pink. "We drive through the Haight every weekend," Caroline's mother said. "Just looking." She was pale and controlled. "If you should see her, would you tell her to call?"

I would not. I made one attempt to return one little boy to his family, and look what happened. Either Sergeant Redburn jumped from the Golden Gate Bridge in the middle of his investigation or he didn't. Either Paul Becker died in Mercy Hospital or he was picked up by the military to be their special weapon in a special war.

I've thought about it now for a couple of decades, and I've decided that, at least for Paul, once he'd escaped from the military, things didn't work out so badly. He must have felt more at home in the tunnels under Cu Chi than he had under the bed in Mercy Hospital.

There is a darkness inside us all that is animal. Against some things—untreated or untreatable disease, for example, or old age—the darkness is all we are. Either we are strong enough animals or we are not. Such things pare everything that is not animal away from us. As animals we have a physical value, but in moral terms we are neither good nor bad. Morality begins on the way back from the darkness.

The first two plagues were largely believed to be a punishment for man's sinfulness. "So many died," wrote Agnolo di Tura the Fat, who buried all five of his own children himself, "that all believed that it was the end of the world." This being the case, you'd imagine the cessation of the plague must have been accompanied by outbreaks of charity and godliness. The truth was just the opposite. In 1349, in Erfurt, Germany, of the three thousand Jewish residents there, not one survived. This is a single instance of a barbarism so marked and so pervasive, it can be understood only as a form of mass insanity.

Here is what Procopius said: *And after the plague had ceased, there was so much depravity and general licentiousness, that it seemed as though the disease had left only the most wicked.*

When men are turned into animals, it's hard for them to find their way back to themselves. When children are turned into animals, there's no self to find. There's never been a feral child who found his way out of the dark. Maybe there's never been a feral child who wanted to.

You don't believe I saw Paul in the tunnels at all. You think I'm crazy or, charitably, that I was crazy then, just for a little while. Maybe you think the CIA would never have killed a policeman or tried to use a little child in a black war, even though the CIA has done everything else you've ever been told and refused to believe.

That's okay. I like your version just fine. Because if I made him up, and all the tunnel rats who ever saw him made him up, then he belongs to us, he marks us. Our vision, our Procopian phantom in the tunnels. Victor to take care of us in the dark.

Caroline came home without me. I read her wedding announcement in the paper more than twenty years ago. She married a Stanford chemist. There was a picture of her in her parents' backyard with gardenias in her hair. She was twenty-five years old. She looked happy. I never did go talk to her.

So here's a story for you, Caroline:

A small German town was much plagued by rats who ate the crops and the chickens, the ducks, the cloth, and the seeds. Finally the citizens called in an exterminator. He was the best; he trapped and poisoned the rats. Within a month he had deprived the fleas of most of their hosts.

The fleas then bit the children of the town instead. Hundreds of children were taken with a strange dancing and raving disease. Their parents tried to control them, tried to keep them safe in their beds, but the moment their mothers' backs were turned, the children ran into the streets and danced. The town was Erfurt. The year was 1237.

Most of the children danced themselves to death. But not all. A few of them recovered and lived to be grown-ups. They married and worked and had their own children. They lived reasonable and productive lives.

The only thing is that they still twitch sometimes. Just now and then. They can't help it.

Stop me, Caroline, if you've heard this story before.

Always

How I Got Here:

I was seventeen years old when I heard the good news from Wilt Loomis, who had it straight from Brother Porter himself. Wilt was so excited he was ready to drive to the city of Always that very night. Back then I just wanted to be anywhere Wilt was. So we packed up.

Always had two openings, and these were going for five thousand apiece, but Wilt had already talked to Brother Porter, who said, seeing as it was Wilt, who was good with cars, he'd take twenty-five hundred down and give us another three years to come up with the other twenty-five, and let that money cover us both. You average that five thousand, Wilt told me, over the infinite length of your life and it worked out to almost nothing a year. Not exactly nothing, but as close to nothing as you could get without getting to nothing. It was too good a deal to pass up. They were practically paying us.

My stepfather was drinking again, and it looked less and less like I was going to graduate high school. Mother was just as glad to have me out of the house and harm's way. She did give me some advice. You can always tell a cult from a religion, she said, because a cult is just a set of rules that lets certain men get laid.

And then she told me not to get pregnant, which I could have taken as a shot across the bow, her new way of saying her life would have been so much better without me, but I chose not to. Already I was taking the long view.

The city of Always was a lively place then—this was back in 1938—part commune and part roadside attraction, set down in the Santa Cruz mountains with the redwoods all around. It used to rain all winter and be damp all summer, too. Slug weather for those big yellow slugs you never saw anywhere but Santa Cruz. Out in the woods it smelled like bay leaves.

The old Santa Cruz Highway snaked through, and the two blocks right on the road were the part open to the public. People would stop there for a soda—Brother Porter used to brag that he'd invented Hawaiian Punch, though the recipe had been stolen by some gang in Fresno who took the credit for it—and to look us over, whisper about us on their way to the beach. We offered penny peep shows for the adults, because Brother Porter said you ought to know what sin was before you abjured it, and a row of wooden Santa Claus statues for the kids. In our heyday we had fourteen gas pumps to take care of all the gawkers.

Brother Porter founded Always in the early twenties, and most of the other residents were already old when I arrived. That made sense, I guess, that they'd be the ones to feel the urgency, but I didn't expect it and I wasn't pleased. Wilt was twenty-five when we first went to Always. Of course, that too seemed old to me then.

The bed I got had just been vacated by a thirty-two-year-old woman named Maddie Beckinger. Maddie was real pretty. She'd just filed a suit against Brother Porter alleging that he'd promised to star her in a movie called *The Perfect Woman,* and when it opened she was supposed to fly to Rome in a replica of the *Spirit of St. Louis,* only this plane would be called the *Spirit of Love.* She said in her suit that she'd always been more interested in being a movie star than in living forever. Who, she asked, was more immortal than Marlene Dietrich? Brother

Porter hated it when we got dragged into the courts, but, as I was to learn, it did keep happening. Lawyers are forever, Brother Porter used to say.

He'd gotten as far as building a sound stage for the movie, which he hoped he might be able to rent out from time to time, and Smitty LeRoy and the Watsonville Wranglers recorded there, but mainly we used it as a dormitory.

Maddie's case went on for two whole years. During this time she came by occasionally to pick up her mail and tell us all she'd never seen such a collection of suckers as we were. Then one day we heard she'd been picked up in Nevada for passing bad checks, which turned out not to be her first offense. So off she went to the San Quentin instead of to Rome. It seemed like a parable to me, but Brother Porter wasn't the sort who resorted to parables.

Lots of the residents had come in twos like Wilt and me, like animals to the ark, only to learn that there was a men's dormitory and a women's, with Brother Porter living up the hill in his own big house, all by himself and closer to the women's dorm than to the men's. Brother Porter told us right after we got there (though not a second before) that even the married couples weren't to sleep together.

There you go, Mother, was my first thought. Not a cult. Only later it was clarified to me that I would be having sex with Brother Porter and so, not a religion, after all.

Frankie Frye and Eleanor Pillser were the ones who told me. I'd been there just about a week, and then one morning, while we were straightening up our cots and brushing our teeth and whatnot, they just came right out with it. At dinner the night before there'd been a card by my plate, the queen of hearts, which was Brother Porter's signal, only I didn't know that so I didn't go.

Frankie Frye, yes, that Frankie Frye, I'll get to all that, had the cot on one side of me and Eleanor the cot on the other. The dormitory was as dim in the morning as at night on account of also being a sound stage and having no windows. There was just one light dangling from the ceiling, with a chain that didn't reach down far enough, so about a foot of string had been added to it. "The thing the men don't get," Frankie said to me, snapping her pillowcase smooth, "The thing the men mustn't get," Eleanor added on, "is that sleeping with Brother Porter is no hardship," said Frankie.

Frankie was thirty-five then and the postmistress. Eleanor was in her early forties and had come to Always with her husband, Rog. I can't tell you how old Brother Porter was, because he always said he wouldn't give an irrelevant number the power of being spoken out loud. He was a fine-looking man though. A man in his prime.

Wilt and I had done nothing but dry runs so far, and he'd brought me to Always and paid my way into eternity with certain expectations. He was a fine-looking man, too, and I won't say I wasn't disappointed, just that I took the news better than he did. "I can't lie to you," he told me in those few days after he learned he wouldn't be having sex, but before he learned that I would be. "This is not the way I pictured it. I sort of thought with all that extra time, I'd get to be with more people, not less."

And when he did hear about me and Brother Porter, he pointed out that the rest of the world only had to be faithful until death did them part. "I don't care how good he is," Wilt said. "You won't want to be with him and no one else forever." Which I suspected he would turn out to be right about, and he was. But in those early days, Brother Porter could make my pulse dance like a snake in a basket. In those early days, Brother Porter never failed to bring the goods.

We had a lot of tourists back then, especially in the summer. They would sidle up to us in their beach gear, ten-cent barbecue in one hand and skepticism in the other, to ask how we could really be sure Brother Porter had made us immortal. At first I tried to explain that it took two things to be immortal: it took Brother Porter and it took faith in Brother Porter. If I started asking the question, then I was already missing one of the two things it took.

But this in no way ended the matter. You think about hearing the same question a couple hundred times, and then add to that the knowledge that you'll be hearing it forever, because the way some people see it, you could be two hundred and five and then suddenly die when you're two hundred and six. The world is full of people who couldn't be convinced of cold in a snowstorm.

I was made the Always zookeeper. We had a petting zoo, three goats, one llama, a parrot named Parody, a dog named Chowder, and a monkey named Monkeyshines, but Monkeyshines bit and couldn't be let loose among the tourists no matter how much simple pleasure it would have given me to do so.

We immortals didn't leave Always much. We didn't have to; we grew our own food, had our own laundry, tailor, barber (though the lousy haircuts had figured prominently in Maddie's suit), and someone to fix our shoes. At first, Brother Porter discouraged field trips, and then later we just found we had less and less in common with people who were going to die. When I complained about how old everyone else at Always was, Wilt pointed out that I was actually closer in age to some seventy-year-old who, like me, was going to live forever, than to some eighteen-year-old with only fifty or so years left. Wilt was as good with numbers as he was with cars, and he was as right about that as everything else. Though some might go and others with five thousand to slap down might arrive, we were a tight community then, and I felt as comfortable in Always as I'd felt anywhere.

The Starkes were the first I ever saw leave. They were a married couple in their mid-forties. (Evelyn Barton and Harry Capps were in their forties, too. Rog and Eleanor, as I've said. Frankie a bit younger. The rest, and there were about thirty of us all told, were too old to guess at, in my opinion.)

Karen Joy Fowler

The Starkes had managed our radio station, KFQU (which looks nasty, but was really just sequential) until the FRC shut us down, claiming we deviated from our frequency. No one outside Always wanted to hear Brother Porter sermonizing, because no one outside Always thought life was long enough.

The Starkes quit on eternity when Brother Porter took their silver Packard and crashed it on the fishhook turn just outside Los Gatos. Bill Starkes loved that Packard, and even though Brother Porter walked away with hardly a scratch, something about the accident made Bill lose his faith. For someone with all the time in the world, he told us while he waited for his wife to fetch her things, Brother Porter surely does drive fast. (In his defense, Brother Porter did tell the police he wasn't speeding, and he stuck to that. He was just in the wrong lane, he said, for the direction in which he was driving.) (He later said that the Starkes hadn't quit over the crash, after all. They'd been planted as fifth columnists in Always and left because we were all such patriots, they saw there was no point to it. Or else they were about to be exposed. I forget which.)

The next to go were Joseph Fitton and Cleveland March. The men just woke up one morning to find Joe and Cleveland's cots stripped bare and Cleveland's cactus missing from the windowsill, without a word said, but Wilt told me they'd been caught doing something they didn't think was sex, but Brother Porter did.

I couldn't see leaving myself. The thing I'd already learned was that when you remove death from your life, you change everything that's left. Take the petting zoo. Parrots are pretty long-lived compared to dogs and goats, but even they die. I'd been there less than two years when Chowder, our little foxhound, had to be put down because his kidneys failed. He wasn't the first dog I'd ever lost; he was just the first I'd lost since I wasn't dying myself. I saw my life stretching forward, all counted out in dead dogs, and I saw I couldn't manage that.

I saw that my pets from now on would have to be turtles or trees or nothing. Turtles and trees don't engage the way dogs do, but you can only have your heart broken so many times until it just won't mend again. I sat with Chowder and pulled him into my lap as he died and I was crying so hard for all the Chowderless years ahead that I understood then and there that immortality was going to bring a certain coldness, a remoteness into my life. I hadn't expected that, but I didn't see a way out of it.

Here's another thing that changes: your investment strategies. As Wilt would say, we were all about T-bills now. Wilt said that often. I got real tired of Wilt saying that.

How It Went On:

Time passed, and I felt pretty good about my situation. No one at Always died, and this was a powerful persuasion given how very old some of them were. Not that I needed persuading. I wasn't the youngest woman anymore, that was Kitty Strauss, and I didn't get the queen of hearts so often, but that was okay with me. Only the parrot was left from the petting zoo, so you couldn't really call it a zoo now, and I didn't see as much of the tourists and that was okay with me, too.

Three years in, Wilt had decided he'd gone for immortality prematurely. It had occurred to him that the older residents lived their full lives first, and only arrived in Always when they were tired of the flesh. Not that he wanted to wait as long as some. Winnifred spent every meal detailing the sufferings her arthritis caused her, as if we women weren't already listening to her toss and turn and hack and snore all night long.

Also, he hadn't managed to scrape up the second twenty-five hundred dollars we owed, and it wasn't likely he would, since Brother Porter collected all our paychecks as a matter of course.

Karen Joy Fowler

So Wilt told me that he wouldn't ante up again for eternity until he'd slept with at least twenty-five women, but no sooner did he move into San Jose than he was on his way to the Pacific Theater as a mechanic on the USS *Aquarius*. For a while I got postcards from the Gilberts, Marshalls, Marianas, and Carolines. It would have been a real good time for Wilt to be immortal, but if he was thinking that too, he never said it.

In fact, the postcards didn't say much of anything. Maybe this was navy policy, or maybe Wilt remembered that Brother Porter vetted all our mail first. Whichever, Brother Porter handed Wilt's postcards to me without comment, but he read Mother's letters aloud in the dining hall after dinner, especially if someone was in the hospital and not expected to recover or was cheating on her husband or her ration card. I listened just like everyone else, only mildly interested, as if these weren't mostly people I'd once known.

Brother Porter said Mother's letters were almost as good as the *Captain Midnight* radio show, which I guess meant that up in the big house, he had a radio and listened to it. Lots of Mother's friends were being neglected by their children. You might say this was a theme. No one ever needed a secret decoder ring to figure Mother out.

It didn't seem to me that the war lasted all that long, though Wilt felt otherwise. When he got back, I'd meet him from time to time in San Jose and we'd have a drink. The city of Always was dry, except for once when a bunch of reporters in the Fill Your Hole club rented out our dining space, invited us to join them, and spiked the punch so as to get a story from it. It ended in a lot of singing, and Winnifred Allington fell off Brother Porter's porch, and Jeb Porter, Brother Porter's teenage son, punched out Harry Capps as a refutation of positive thinking, but the reporters had left by then, so they missed it all.

Anyway Brother Porter never explicitly made abstention a condition, and I never asked him about it in case he would. I still got my age checked whenever we went to a bar, so that was good. It renewed my faith every time it happened. Not that my faith needed renewing.

Now that Wilt was dying again, our interests had diverged. He was caught up in politics, local corruptions, national scandals. He read the newspapers. He belonged to the auto mechanics' union, and he told me he didn't care that the war had ended so much as I might think. The dead were still dead, and he'd seen way too many of them. He said that war served the purposes of corporations and politicians so exactly that there would always be another one, and then another, until the day some president or prime minister figured out how to declare a war that lasted forever. He said he hoped he'd die before that day came. I wonder sometimes if that worked out for him.

Once, while he was still at Always, Wilt took me to the ocean so that we could stand on the edge and imagine eternity. Now when Wilt talked politics, I'd fill my ears with the sound of the ocean instead. Corporate puppet masters and congressional witch-hunts and union payola—they all drowned together in the pounding of the sea.

Still I went out with Wilt every time he asked. Mostly this was gratitude because he'd bought me eternity. Love had gone the way of the petting zoo for me. Sex was a good thing, and there were plenty of times I couldn't sleep for wanting it. But even if sleeping with Wilt wouldn't have cost my life, I wouldn't have. *There was a match found for me at last.* I fell in love with a shrub oak, I read once in high school in a book about Thoreau, who died more than a hundred years ago and left that shrub oak a grieving widow.

When I first came to Always, there were six Erle Stanley Gardner mysteries in the women's dormitory that used to belong to Maddie. I read them all several times. But I wasn't reading anymore and certainly not murder mysteries. I'd even stopped liking music. I'd always supposed that art was about beauty and that beauty was forever. Now I saw that that music was all about time. You take a photograph and it's all about that moment and how that moment will never come again. You go into a library and every book on the shelves is all about death, even the ones pretending to be about birth or rebirth or resurrection or reincarnation.

Only the natural world is rendered eternal. Always was surrounded by the Santa Cruz Mountains, which meant tree trunks across streams, ghostly bear prints deep inside the forest, wild berries, tumbles of rocks, mosses, earthquakes, and storms. Out behind the post office was a glade where Brother Porter gave his sermons, had sex, and renewed our lifespans. It was one of those rings of redwoods made when the primary tree in the center dies. Brother Porter had us brick a wall in a half circle behind the trees so it would be more churchlike, and the trees grew straight as candles; you could follow along their trunks all the way to the stars. The first time Brother Porter took me there and I lay smelling the loam and the bay (and also Brother Porter) and looking up, I thought to myself that no matter how long I lived, this place would always be beautiful to me.

I talked less and less. At first, my brain tried to make up the loss, dredging up random flashes from my past—advertising slogans, old songs, glimpses of shoes I'd worn, my mother's jewelry, the taste of an ant I'd once eaten. A dream I'd had in which I was surrounded by food that was bigger than me, bread slices the size of mattresses, which seems like it should have been a good dream, but it wasn't. Memories fast and scattershot. It pleased me to think my last experience of mortality would be a toothpaste commercial. Good-bye to all that.

Then I smoothed out, and days would go by when it seemed I hardly thought at all. Tree time.

So it wasn't just Wilt. I was finding it harder to relate to people in general, and, no, this is not a complaint. I never minded having so little in common with those outside Always and their revved-up, streaming-by lives.

While inside Always, I already knew what everyone was going to say.

1) Winnifred was going to complain about her arthritis.

2) John was going to tell us that we were in for a cold winter. He'd make it sound like he was just reading the signs, like he had all this lore, the fuzzy caterpillars coming early or being especially fuzzy or some such thing. He was going to remind us that he hadn't always lived in California, so he knew what a cold winter really was. He was going to say that Californians didn't know cold weather from their asses.

3) Frankie was going to say that it wasn't her job to tape our mail shut for us and she wasn't doing it anymore; we needed to bring it already taped.

4) Anna was going to complain that her children wouldn't talk to her just because she'd spent their inheritance on immortality. That their refusal to be happy for her was evidence that they'd never loved her.

5) Harry was going to tell us to let a smile be our umbrella.

6) Brother Porter was going to wonder why the arcade wasn't bringing in more money. He was going to add that he wasn't accusing any of us of pocketing, but that it did make you wonder how all those tourists could stop and spend so little money.

7) Kitty was going to tell us how many boys in the arcade had come on to her that day. Her personal best was seventeen. She would make this sound like a problem.

8) Harry would tell us to use those lemons and make lemonade.

9) Vincent was going to say that he thought his watch was fast and make everyone else still wearing a watch tell him what time they had. The fact that the times would vary minutely never ceased to interest him and was good for at least another hour of conversation.

10) Frankie was going to say that no one ever listened to her.

Karen Joy Fowler

It was a kind of conversation that required nothing in response. On and on it rolled, like the ocean.

Wilt always made me laugh, and that never changed either, only it took me so much longer to get the joke. Sometimes I'd be back at Always before I noticed how witty he'd been.

What Happened Next:

Here's the part you already know. One day one spring—one day when the Canada geese were passing overhead yet again, and we were out at the arcades, taking money from tourists, and I was thrilling for the umpteenth time to the sight of the migration, the chevron, the honking, the sense of a wild, wild spirit in the air—Brother Porter took Kitty out to the cathedral ring and he died there.

At first Kitty thought she'd killed him by making the sex so exciting, though anyone else would have been tipped off by the frothing and the screaming. The police came and they shermanned their way through Always. Eventually they found a plastic bag of rat poison stuffed inside one of the unused post-office boxes and a half-drunk cup of Hawaiian Punch on the mail scale that tested positive for it.

Inside Always, we all got why it wasn't murder. Frankie Frye reminded us that she had no way of suspecting it would kill him. She was so worked up and righteous, she made the rest of us feel we hadn't ever had the same faith in Brother Porter she'd had or we would have poisoned him ourselves years ago.

But no one outside of Always could see this. Frankie's lawyers refused to plead it out that way; they went with insanity and made all the inner workings of Always part of their case. They dredged up the old string of arsons as if they were relevant, as if they hadn't stopped entirely the day Brother Porter finally threw his son out on his ear. Jeb was a witness for the prosecution, and a more angelic face you never saw. In retrospect, it was a great mistake to have given immortality to a fourteen-year-old boy. When he had it, he was a jerk, and I could plainly see that not having it had only made him an older jerk.

Frankie's own lawyers made such a point of her obesity that they reduced her to tears. It was a shameful performance and showed how little they understood us. If Frankie ever wished to lose weight, she had all the time in the world to do so. There was nothing relevant or even interesting in her weight.

The difficult issue for the defense was whether Frankie was insane all by herself or along with all the rest of us. Sometimes they seemed to be arguing the one and sometimes the other, so when they chose not to call me to the stand I didn't know if this was because I'd make us all look more crazy or less so. Kitty testified nicely. She charmed them all and the press dubbed her the Queen of Hearts at her own suggestion.

Wilt was able to sell his three years among the immortals to a magazine and recoup every cent of that twenty-five hundred he put up for me. There wasn't much I was happy about right then, but I was happy about that. I didn't even blame him for the way I came off in the article. I expect coquettish was the least I deserved. I'd long ago stopped noticing how I was behaving at any given moment.

I would have thought the trial would be just Mother's cup of tea, even without me on the witness stand, so I was surprised not to hear from her. It made me stop and think back, try to remember when her last letter had come. Could have been five years, could have been ten. Could have been twenty, could have been two. I figured she must be dead, which was bound to happen sooner or later, though I did think she was young to go, but that might only have been because I'd lost track of how old she was. I never heard from her again, so I think I had it right. I wonder if it was the cigarettes. She always said that smoking killed germs.

Not one of the immortals left Always during the trial. Partly we were in shock and huddled up as a result. Partly there was so much to be done, so much money to be made.

The arcade crawled with tourists and reporters, too. Looking for a story, but also, as always, trying to make one. "Now that Brother Porter is dead," they would ask, exact wording to change, but point always the same, "don't you have some doubts? And if you have some doubts, well, then, isn't the game already over?" They were tiresome, but they paid for their Hawaiian Punch just like everyone else, and we all knew Brother Porter wouldn't have wanted them kept away.

Frankie was let off by reason of insanity. Exactly two days later Harry Capps walked into breakfast just when Winnifred Allington was telling us how badly she'd slept the night before on account of her arthritis. By the time he ran out of bullets, four more immortals were dead.

Harry's defense was no defense. "Not one of them ever got a good night's sleep," he said. "Someone had to show them what a good night's sleep was."

The politicians blamed the overly-lenient Frankie Frye verdict for the four new deaths and swore the same mistake would not be made twice. Harry got life.

Why I'm Still Here:

Everyone else either died or left and now I'm the whole of it. The last of the immortals; City of Always, population one. I moved up to the big house, and I'm the postmistress now, along with anything else I care to keep going. I get a salary from the government with benefits and a pension they'll regret if I live forever. They have a powerful faith I won't.

The arcade is closed except for the peep shows, which cost a quarter now and don't need me to do anything to run them but collect the coins after. People don't come through so much since they built the 17, but I still get customers from time to time. They buy a postcard and they want the Always postmark on it.

Wilt came to fetch me after the noise died down. "I brought you here," he said. "Seems like I should take you away." He never did understand why I wouldn't leave. He hadn't lived here long enough to understand it.

I tried the easy answer first. I got shot by Harry Capps, I said. Right through the heart. Was supposed to die. Didn't.

But then I tried again, because that wasn't the real answer and if I'd ever loved anyone, I'd loved Wilt. Who'll take care of the redwoods if I go? I asked him. Who'll take care of the mountains? He still didn't get it, though he said he did. I wouldn't have known how to leave even if I'd wanted to. What I was and what he was—they weren't the same thing at all anymore. There was no way back to what I'd been. The actual living forever part? That was always, always the least of it.

Which is the last thing I'm going to say on the subject. There is no question you can ask I haven't already answered and answered and answered again. Time without end.

Familiar Birds

Between the ages of eight and fifteen, I was packed off to the seaside for a month every summer to stay with the Hutching family. Norma Hutching had been my mother's college roommate. She had three children—two boys considerably older than me with whom I had almost nothing to do, and one girl, Daisy, only one year my elder. Since I had lived most of my life in a house with a television and a city with a sports franchise, you might have thought I had things to say worth listening to. You didn't know Daisy. She always acted as if she'd packed a lot of learning into that extra year she had on me.

Daisy's mother ran a seafood restaurant, and her father a charter fishing boat. My mother would join us most weekends, sometimes with my father, when his job permitted. The Hutchings weren't rich enough to live at the beach with their tourist clientele, but had a house half an hour away in woody seclusion. It was a property littered with thorns, bugs, and birds. Daisy became my self-appointed docent to the natural world.

"This tree," Daisy would say—she took me around the property every year on the day I arrived to remind me that I was on her turf now—"is older than Columbus." Which made me wonder, first, how she could know this, and, second, how old Columbus was. Do you keep counting after you die?

There was no point in asking. Daisy, while more than generous with her information if allowed to offer it spontaneously, would answer no questions. I'd had teachers like that. To their way of thinking, questions expressed less interest than doubt. (To be fair, as far as my questions went, this was often accurate.)

"We used to have lots of bees here when I was little," Daisy said. "They all died of a stomach parasite.

"Those leaves have five fingers, just like a hand. That's why they call them finger-leaves. Some word that means finger-leaves.

"Every seven years you get a whole new skin. Everything on the outside of you, everything you see, is already dead." Daisy poked me with the sharp corner of her fingernail. "Dead person," she said.

I spent these summers trying to get the upper hand. At my school I was quite likely to win a spelling bee, have the best birthday party, sing the solo for the Christmas concert. I could see that Daisy, dropped into that competitive environment, would be no one. I would have liked it if Daisy had seen this, too, but it was a hard point to make on her home ground. I spent my summers bossed about by someone to whom, anywhere else, anywhere real, I was clearly superior.

Sometimes we went with Mrs. Hutching to the restaurant. If she was short-staffed, we'd be asked to stamp the restaurant name (Crow's Nest) on pats of butter, fold the napkins into the wine glasses. When we were done, we'd hang about the pier. If there were tourist kids around—there usually were—I'd make it plain that I didn't live here, either. Daisy had hard little eyes, eyes like buttons. I'd feel them on me, but I didn't care. Down by the pier, I'd be the one doing the talking.

Have I been clear? I didn't like Daisy and she didn't like me and this was because neither one of us was likable. Anyone but our mothers would have seen that straight off. But they liked each other so much, our friendship was compulsory. "Our Daisy," my mother would say appreciatively. "She is one smart little girl." Just because Daisy'd once said she preferred a good book to any television show. I actually laughed when she said this, and even laughing didn't tip my mother off to the fact that she was being played, only to the fact that I was being rude.

"I wish," Daisy's mother would tell Daisy, "that you had the manners Clara has." Clara being me. And all I had done was thank Mrs. Hutching for the meal she'd made, tell her it was good. I hadn't even eaten the food. You had to wonder sometimes just how smart our mothers were.

"You can't drink the stream water here," Daisy said. "There are eggs in it, and if you swallow them, they hatch into worms that live in your gut. Down by the Columbus tree the water's cleaner, because it's just gone over the rocks. The rocks scrape the eggs out of it.

"When you find three stones piled up like that, it means, danger. Beware. The Indians used to do that. Some of the stone piles around here are from Indian times.

"That bird there built a nest last year in the porch eaves. It was a lousy nest. All the eggs dropped right through and smashed on the porch. Birds can go crazy, just like people. That one has. She's like those old ladies you see in the city in their ratty old sweaters, talking to themselves."

Daisy's recurring themes: you'll die here, because you don't know what you're doing.

And the city is lousy, too.

The year I was eleven Daisy explained to me how she came to know so much about nature. She said that it spoke to her. She had conversations with birds and trees, just exactly the same as she did with people. They could talk to anyone, those birds, those trees. But mostly they didn't want to. They had to really trust you.

I was immediately suspicious. I'd caught Daisy in lies before (look at that ridiculous one about not liking television) and this, if true, seemed too big a secret to have kept so long. Besides, why her?

But I didn't tell anyone what she'd said, either, not right off, and since I so liked to make her look bad this is harder to explain. The best I can do is this: I was the kind of child who scraped the frosting from my Oreos, eating only the cookies until I'd collected a whole ball of frosting, which I then ate all at once. Daisy was the kind who ate her frosting first and then tried to make a deal for yours. Daisy was not the sort to save something good for later. I was.

"The Mormons used to make tea from this," Daisy said. She was pointing to a particularly leggy, stickery plant. "They picked the leaves and dried them and then put them in boiling water. They thought this tea stopped pregnancies. Any woman found with the dried leaves was excommunicated. Or thrown into prison.

"We have cougars here sometimes," Daisy said. "They hunt in packs, and they always pick the smallest, weakest person as their prey."

Daisy outweighed me by a good twenty pounds.

The property only looked beautiful to me when I went around it with my mother. Then I would see the reflections of trees laid upside down on the water and rippling; the tiny rainbows woven into an insect's wing; a black feather floating like a boat between two stones.

When my mother stayed, she slept on a futon in the Hutchings' living room. If I managed to stay awake long enough, I'd leave the bedroom Daisy and I shared and join my mother. "Do you think there are people birds talk to?" I asked her, that year I was eleven. I was lying in, close as I could get, one of her arms under me and one arm over.

I'd been reading *The Secret Garden* and had decided that loving the land reflected better on me than feeling slightly menaced whenever I went out. I'd thought of Daisy when I read how Dicken spoke to the birds, how the robin brought Mary the lost garden key. I wanted to be the kind of child birds brought keys to rather than the kind of child cougars picked off and ate. Loving nature in all her aspects seemed to me the first step in switching over.

"When I was a little girl," my mother said, "we had a parakeet. It knew several words, but it also used to babble sort of sleepily to itself for hours at a time."

"Wild birds, I meant," I said.

"My arm's going to sleep. Move off a minute." My mother rolled me away and then rolled me back. "Anyway. I wasn't done with my story. My grandmother lived in Germany and I hadn't seen her for three years when we heard she'd suddenly died. My mother cried so hard and so long. She lay on the couch for days, weeks it seemed to me, facedown in a pillow, and if you touched her or tried to talk she said to please, please just leave her be. We even had the doctor in to see her.

"One day when she'd been lying on the couch, she suddenly sat up gasping. The parakeet had been babbling away and then said something absolutely clear, but in German. 'Don't cry, little dearest. It's beautiful here,' the bird said.

"Now, that bird didn't learn anything without you saying it over and over and over. Mother figured Grandma must have been working with it ever since she died."

"Did it scare you?" I asked. I would have been scared to think my dead grandma was in the house. Or anyone's dead grandma.

"It made Mother stop crying. I was much more scared when I thought she was never going to stop," my mother answered.

There was another reason I didn't tell my mother about the claims Daisy had made. Whenever I tried to complain about Daisy, my mother anticipated me, headed me off. She did this in a cunning way, by telling me she was proud of me. "Daisy doesn't have as many friends as you," she would say. "Living here, so out of the way, I think she's very lonely. I know she irritates you sometimes. Even good friends can really annoy each other. But you're always so sweet to her. It makes me very proud to see.

"Norma says Daisy spends all year waiting for summer, when you come back," my mother said.

The whole arrangement worked so well for our parents. Daisy's parents could go off to work confident they'd left Daisy with company and things to do. Mine avoided the summer daycare problem, provided me with the benefits of brothers and sisters, and took a holiday from parenting themselves. No one was going to let a little thing like Daisy's and my mutual antipathy spoil all this.

My mother went back to the city. The weather improved. The tourists packed the road to the beach so you could hardly get to the store for milk without it taking the afternoon. Mr. and Mrs. Hutching left early and came home late and exhausted. Mr. Hutching's nose had turned bright red and was now peeling.

They were less likely to bring Daisy and me to the beach, now that the workday was so long and hard. On July 4th they made an exception. Mr. Hutching was taking some tourists out in the evening so they could see the fireworks from the water. There'd be a picnic on the boat: potato salad, five-bean salad, hamburgers and hot-dogs. He'd barbecue any fish they caught. Daisy and I could come along, he said, and help.

The tourists turned out to be two families. There were four children—a two-year-old, two fives, and a seven. You'd think I'd find it beneath me, playing my usual game to such an easy audience. You'd be wrong. I told the children Daisy talked to birds.

"I never said that," Daisy said.

"We should call her birdbrain," I suggested. "But only when the grown-ups can't hear. Can you all do that? Are you big enough to do that?"

"Birdbrain," said one of the fives.

I'd held off on the really good card. Now I played it. "She talks to trees, too."

"Treebrain!" the seven said. We were all having fun now. Daisy went up to stand at the tiller with her father.

A gull landed on the deck rail. "Birdbrain's not here," I told it. Much hilarity. "Can I take a message?" The gull turned sideways to look at me with one red-ringed eye. It puffed out its feathers, and then shuffled them back into place. Flapped its wings, stretched its neck, but didn't fly. I didn't like the way it was looking at me.

Too late I remembered my plan to be the sort of child birds brought keys to. I tried to rewind. "We won't really call Daisy birdbrain," I told the children, who were disappointed to hear it. "I just made that stuff up about the birds and the trees."

Of course, Daisy wasn't there for this. She was scolded later for leaving all the babysitting to me. "One of you was very helpful yesterday," Daisy's father said.

The next day, Daisy worked to reestablish her supremacy. "July is snake month here," she told me. "I hope you brought your anti-venom. I don't need any, myself. If you live around here, you get shots.

"My father is going to build a tree house for me. For when I want to be alone. No one else will ever be allowed inside it. We're just picking out the right tree.

"Your mother isn't coming down this weekend. I don't know why. I guess she's too busy or sick or something. Germs spread much faster

Karen Joy Fowler

in the city because you're all crammed up against each other. All it takes is one person coughing on the bus.

"My mother says your mother never really wanted children. She had her tubes tied after you were born.

"See those two little birds flying at the one big one? Birds do that. They join together to pester any bird bigger and faster than they are. It's called mobbing."

We were walking down to the creek, single file. A sparrow landed in a nearby tree, hopped along the branch. "That's a white-crowned sparrow," Daisy told me. "What's that?" she asked it. "No, she's from the city. No, she's staying all summer." And then to me again, "He wishes you'd go home."

This fooled no one. But the whole time Daisy talked, the woods were filled with bird noise. I'd never heard so much of it before, or maybe I'd never listened so carefully. There was a bird with a call like a clicking tongue. The round, hollow sound of a dove. A nearby trill, a faraway whistle. A loose flock of ducks passed over us, white sides, narrow red bills, hoarse croaking cries. Last winter, two girls in my class had decided they didn't like me. They would lean together, whispering, whenever I passed. I had the same feeling now, that I was being talked about behind my back and nothing good was being said.

That afternoon my mother phoned. "Did Norma tell you I can't make this weekend, sweetie?" she asked. "I've got a report due in to accounting. I'm just swamped. I may not get there next weekend, either, just giving you a heads-up. Lucky you! Out in the country without a care in the world!"

The year I turned fifteen was the only year Daisy ever came to stay with us. She came just after Christmas, just about the time she started showing. She refused to say who the father was, but probably some tourist boy, her parents guessed, because of the timing. It was a thing that happened to the local girls, though they'd certainly never expected their Daisy.

Her father thought it might be a boy in her class, because suddenly she was throwing a fit about going to school. They had just about had it with her. Clara would never, they assured my parents. Your Clara is too smart for this.

My parents immediately offered our home: they loved Daisy. So now it was my bedroom we shared, and I went off to class each morning, but she stayed behind, promising everyone she would make it up in summer school. She settled onto our living-room couch and did nothing but watch television and get bigger.

By this time Daisy and I had wearied of our hostilities. We still didn't like each other, but the whole thing was pasted over with a thin politeness. I was trying to be a better person in general. It has never come naturally, but I do try.

The first night before we went to sleep, Daisy told me how much the baby's father loved her. He was, she said, a really, really good-looking guy who wanted to marry her. But she wasn't sure it was in her best interest.

She was the one who'd advised him to stay away, keep his mouth shut, and she made me promise that, if a boy ever called for her, I would say he had the wrong number. Right now he was probably searching high and low for her, and she wasn't sure her brothers could be trusted not to say where she was.

A little while later we learned that the baby was a boy. That night I woke and heard her crying. I pretended to sleep until the crying got so loud I was sure I was supposed to hear it.

"What's wrong?" I asked.

She told me that, back when she'd first thought she might be pregnant, she'd tried to get rid of the baby with the Mormon tea.

She was crying so hard, at first I could barely understand her.

There'd been no time to dry the leaves, which is maybe why it hadn't worked. But the tea had made her throw up, and ever since, she was afraid she might have hurt the baby. The Hutchings didn't believe in abortion. Daisy had no one but me to tell, and I wasn't to say a word to anyone, though, she said, when the baby was born with no hands or no brain everyone would figure it out.

I was surprised to be confided in, and I said what I hoped was the right thing, that I was sure everything would be okay. But how could I know? Things were already not okay.

The Hutchings didn't believe in abortion, nor would they let Daisy raise her own child. The baby was already promised to a family in the city, a Beck and Melody Marshke. The Marshkes called twice a week to see how Daisy was feeling, make sure she was eating fresh vegetables, red meats. Organic milk. Of course, no alcohol. No smoking.

"Daisy wants to keep her baby," I told my mother. Daisy had, in fact, said this once (but only once). Mostly I thought she *should* want to keep him. "I don't see why it's not up to her."

"Daisy doesn't know what raising a child involves. She's still a child herself. She's a smart girl with a bright future ahead. Her parents want her to have her own childhood before she's saddled with her own children." And then, running out of clichés, "You could be nicer to her," my mother said, when it seemed to me I had been nothing but nice.

But maybe not. Daisy and my mother were thick as thieves now and I never cared for that. They commiserated over the apparently perfectly natural horrors of exhaustion, insomnia, nausea, hormonal upsets, acne, swollen breasts. Pregnancy had become Daisy's new expertise, the new thing she knew all about and me nothing. "You can't even imagine," she would say to me. "You're so lucky not to even know." Once again nature and Daisy had managed to one-up me.

—m—

The baby arrived in early May. I had to go to school as usual, and when I came home, things still hadn't finished. The Hutchings had driven over, eighty the whole way, Norma told us, but there turned out to be plenty of time. Daisy was in labor for thirty-four hours.

Mother came home twice to eat and then went straight back to the hospital. By the time the baby arrived, everyone was exhausted. Mother called to give us the news. "A big healthy boy," she said. "Just beautiful! Perfect in every detail."

His parents took him away. Daisy's parents took her home. I never saw him.

For a long time I carried the Marshkes' address in my coat pocket. I'd gotten it off the internet, nothing simpler, and I knew how to get there—the 42 bus and then a transfer to the 18. The thought that I could go anytime was a good one, though I never did.

Since then, I wonder about every boy I pass, every boy of a certain age. There they are, two of them, three of them, they're four years old, they're ten, now they're fifteen and flocking to the mall where they bum cigarettes off strangers and brag loudly about how fucked up they got the night before. I wonder where their mothers are.

When she was still at our house, when she was still pregnant, it was my job to get Daisy to her appointments with the obstetrician. My mother couldn't bear to think of her, poor pregnant country girl, on the bus by herself. What if she missed her stop? What if we lost her somehow in the big city? I only thought of this later, that perhaps she was afraid Daisy would run away.

To get to the bus stop, Daisy and I walked across a park with pigeons and sparrows and crows. There were bushes with a kind of berry Daisy said they also had in the country. The berries fall off in the autumn and ferment on the ground, Daisy told me. The birds eat the berries and get drunk. They keel over. When they try to fly, they can't go in a straight line, can't gain any altitude. She was worried, Daisy said, about all those drunken birds in the city. She was afraid they'd fly into the street, get hit by cars.

Private Grave 9

Every week Ferhid takes our trash out and buries it. Last week's included chicken bones, orange peels, a tin that cherries had come in and another for peas, an empty silver-bromide bottle, my used razor-blade, a bakelite comb someone sat on and broke, and several early drafts of Mallick's letter to Lord Wallis about our progress. Mean-while, at G4 and G5, two bone hairpins and seven clay shards were unearthed, one of which was painted with some sort of dog, or so Davis says, though I'd have guessed lion. There's more to be found in other sectors, but all of it too recent—anything Roman or later is still trash to us. G4 and G5 are along the deep cut, and we're finding our oldest stuff there.

I'd spent the morning in the darkroom, ostensibly to work but really because I was tired of the constant gabble of the expedition house. When I grew up, it was just my mother and me. I had the whole third floor to myself, and she wasn't allowed to come up unless I asked her. I've got no gripe against anyone here. It's just a question of what you're used to.

The photographs I was printing were all of infant skeletons. There's an entire level of these, laid out identically on their sides with their legs pulled into their stomachs. Davis had cleared each tiny skull and ribcage with his breath because they were so delicate, and it took a week because there were so many. That seemed very intimate to me, and I wondered if he'd felt any attachment to one more than another. I thought it would probably be rude to ask. My pictures were of all different babies, but all my pictures looked the same.

At lunch, I shared some philosophical thoughts—all about how much sadder finding a single child would have been and how odd that was, you feeling less with each addition.

Mallick, our director, said when I'd put in a few more seasons I'd find I didn't think of them as dead people at all, but as the bead necklace or the copper bowl or whatever else might be found with the body. Mallick's eyes are all rimmed in red like a basset hound's. This gives him a tragic demeanor, when he's really quite cheerful. The whole time he was speaking, Miss Jackson, his secretary, was seated just past him with her head down, attending to her food. Miss Jackson lost her husband in the trenches and her son to the flu after.

Remembering that, and remembering how each of her losses was merely one among so many they might as well have been stars in the sky, made me wish I'd kept my thoughts to myself. Women take death harder than we men. Or that's been my experience.

"No signs of illness or malformation." Davis has a face round as a moon and that pale skin that takes color easily; he's always either blanching or blushing. I watched him clean his fork on his napkin with the same surgical precision, the same careful attention, he brought to every task. Sunlight flashed off the square lenses of his spectacles whenever he looked up at me. Flash, flash, flash. "Best guess?" he said. "Infanticide."

Ferhid had carved us a cold lamb for lunch and had the mail lying under our forks. Ferhid has the profile of a film star, but a mouth full of rotted teeth. His mouth is a painful thing to see, and I wish he didn't smile so often.

We each had a letter or two, which was fair and friendly, though most of them mentioned Howard Carter's dig, which was not. Mine, of course, was from my mother, pretending not to miss me as unpersuasively as she possibly can. I missed the war as her sole support, but since that ended it's been more of a burden. Last month I wrote to her that a man must have a vocation and if nothing comes to him, then he must go looking. Today she responded by wondering if it was necessary to travel half a globe and 4500 years away. She said that Mesopotamia must be about as far from Michigan as it's possible to get. How wonderful, she said, to be so unattached that you can pick up and go anywhere and never mind the people you've left behind. And then she promised me that she wasn't complaining.

Patwin read bits of the *Times* aloud while we had our coffee. Apparently reporters are still camped at the Tut-ankh-Amen tomb, cataloguing gold masks and lapis-lazuli scarabs and ebony effigies as fast as Carter can haul them out. These *Times* accounts have Lord Wallis and everyone else in a spin, as if we're playing some sort of tennis match against Carter and losing badly. Our potsherds, never mind how old they are, have become an embarrassing return on Wallis' investment, though they were good enough before. Our skeletons are too numerous to be tasteful. I'm betting Wallis won't be whimsical about paintings of dogs, nor will anyone else at his club.

As he read, Patwin's tone conveyed his disapproval. He has the darting eyes of an anarchist (and a beard like Freud's), but he's actually a stolid Marxist. So he'll tell you slavery was a necessary historical phase, but it's clear that shards of good clay working-class pots suit him better than golden bowls put by for the afterlife.

"We had a lovely morning in PG 9," Mallick said stoutly. PG stands for private grave, and PG 9 is the largest tomb we've found so far, four chambers in all, and never plundered—naturally, that's the part that has us most excited. A woman is laid out in the second of

Karen Joy Fowler

these chambers—a priestess or a queen in a coffin of clay. There's a necklace of gold leaves and a gold ring. Several of the colored beads she once wore in her hair have fallen into her skull. The skeletons of seven other women, presumably her servants, are kneeling in the third and fourth chambers, along with two groomsmen, two oxen, and a musician with what I imagine, when Davis reconstructs it, will be a lyre. Once upon a time Wallis would have been entirely content with this. A royal tomb. A sleeping priestess. But that was before Carter began to swim in golden sarcophagi.

Another American, a girl from Rapid City, has come to visit us in the mud-brick expedition house. Her name is Emily Whitfield, and she's a cousin of Mallick's wife or a second cousin or some such thing, some relative Mallick found impossible to send away. She's twenty-nine, just a couple years shy of me, flapper haircut, eyes of a washed-out blue, but a good figure. Already there'd been some teasing. "High time you met the right girl," Mallick had said, but the minute I'd seen Miss Whitfield I'd known she wasn't that. I've never believed in love at first sight, but I've had a fair amount of experience with the opposite.

Patwin had claimed to dread Miss Whitfield's visit, in spite of the obvious appeal of a new face. "She'll need to be taken everywhere, and someone will always be hurting her feelings," Patwin had predicted, fingers scratching through his beard. Patwin prided himself on knowing women, although when that would have happened I really couldn't say. "She'll find it all very dirty and our facilities insupportable. She'll never have stood before." And then Patwin had a coughing fit; it was such a rude thing to have said in Miss Jackson's presence.

But Miss Whitfield was proving entirely game. Davis took her to see the baby skeletons, and he said she made no comment, lit an unmoved cigarette. Apparently she's an authoress and quite successful, according to Mallick who'd learned it from his wife. Four books so far, books in which people are killed in clever and unusual ways, murderers unmasked by people even cleverer. She was about to set a book at a dig such as ours; it's why she'd come. Mallick told me to take her along and show her the new tomb, so she was there when I took my picture. I'd been pointing out an arresting detail or two—the way the workmen chant as they haul the rubble out of the chamber, the rags they tie around their heads, their seeping eyes—but she didn't seem interested.

We brought the smell of sweat and flesh with us into the tomb. Most people would have instinctively lowered their voices. Not Miss Whitfield. "I thought it would be grander," she said when we were inside the second chamber. Patwin had rigged an electrical installation so there was plenty of light for our work here. "I didn't picture mud." She lifted a hand to her hair, and when she lowered it again there was a streak of dust running from the hairline down her temple. It gave her a friendlier, franker look, but like Mallick's sad eyes, this proved deceiving. What she really wanted to know was whether there were tensions in the expedition house. "You all live in each other's pockets. It must drive you crazy sometimes. There must be little, annoying habits that send you right around the bend."

"Actually things go very smoothly," I told her. "Sorry to disappoint." I was taking my first photographs of the bones in the coffin, adjusting the lighting, dragging a stool about and standing on it to get the best angle. Miss Whitfield was beneath my elbow. Davis was in a corner of the chamber on his knees, pouring hot wax and pressing a cloth down on it. When the wax dried, he would lift out bits of shell and stone without disturbing their placement.

Miss Whitfield finally softened her voice. She was so close I could smell the cigarette smoke in her hair. "But if you did murder someone," she whispered, "would it more likely be Mr. Patwin or Mr.

Davis?" She might have been asking this at the exact moment I took my first picture.

With her free hand, she reached into the coffin, straight into my second shot, ruining it. I watched through the rangefinder as she rolled the skull slightly away. I was too surprised to stop her. "Please don't touch!" Davis called in alarm from his corner, and she removed her hand.

"I heard Tut-ankh-Amen's head was bashed in at the back with a blunt instrument," she explained. Her smoke-filled disappointment wafted through the tomb. I came off my stool, tried to set the skull back the way it had been, but I couldn't be sure I'd done it right. I'd need to check my first photograph for that.

That night Patwin complained that I was blocking his light while he tried to read. I told him it was interesting that he thought the light belonged to him. I said, that's an interesting point of view for a Marxist to take, and I saw Miss Whitfield pull out her notebook to write the whole thing down.

Next day, a cylindrical seal was found on the bier, and Davis deciphered a name from it, Tu-api, along with a designation for a highborn woman. A princess, not a priestess, then. We also found a golden amulet, carved in the shape of a goat standing on its hind legs. There'd been a second goat, a matching partner, but that one was crushed beyond mending. Pictures of all the ornaments had to be finished in a rush and sent off to Lord Wallis. The goat is really lovely, and my photograph showed it well; no one will have to apologize for that find.

Even better were the stones and shells that Davis had impressed. Mallick believed they'd once been two sides of a wooden box, which had disintegrated, leaving only the pattern.

One side had shown scenes from ordinary life. There was a banquet with guests and musicians, farmers with wood on their backs, oxen and sheep. The second side was all armies, prisoners of war, chariots, men with weapons. Before and After, Miss Jackson called it, but Mallick called it Peace and War to clarify that it represented two parts of a cycle, and not a sequence, that peace would follow war as well as precede it. The unknown artist must have been remarkable, as the people were so detailed, right down to the sorry look on the prisoners' faces.

Patwin criticized me for taking more pictures of Tu-api than of the kneeling girls or the groomsmen or the poor musician. He said that I must fight the bourgeois impulse to care more about the princess than about the slave. It would be even harder, he conceded, now that the princess had a name. But Tu-api, he guessed, had the good fortune to die of natural causes. Unlike the others in her tomb.

"Does he always lecture at you like that?" Miss Whitfield asked. "How irritating that must be!"

Because I was busy developing prints of golden goats and verdigris bowls, because we'd already sent Lord Wallis plenty of photographs of skeletons, I left my pictures of Tu-api untouched for a couple of days. It was late at night when I finally put them through the wash and hung them up, and I didn't look closely until the following morning. In my first shot, Tu-api had a face. This wasn't part of the picture exactly, but a cloudy, ghostly spot with imploring eyes superimposed over the skull. It made my skin crawl up the back of my neck, and I took it out to the dig to show the others. It was a hot day and the air so dry it stung to breathe. I found Mallick, Davis, and Miss Jackson all together in the third chamber around the pit where the oxen had been found.

They were not as unnerved as I was. A human face is an easy thing to find, Davis pointed out, in the paint on a ceiling, the grain in a wooden board. "I once saw the face of God in the clouds," Miss Jackson agreed. "I know how that sounds, but it was as sharp and perfect as a Michelangelo. Sober and very beautiful. Thin Chinese sort of beard. I got down on my knees and watched until it melted and blew away."

This sudden display of fancy from solid, cylindrical Miss Jackson obviously embarrassed Mallick. He got scholarly in response, with his dry voice and those red-rimmed eyes. "I've heard of bodies preserved right down to the facial expression," he said. "In the Arctic ice, for example. Or at very high altitudes. I've always imagined those discoveries to be rather grim."

"Buried in the bogs," Patwin said. He'd arrived with Miss Whitfield while Mallick was speaking. He held out his hand for my photograph and looked it over silently. He handed it to Miss Whitfield. "I knew a man who'd met a man who'd found a thousand-year-old woman while digging for peat. He said you can't look into a thousand-year-old face and not find yourself just a little bit in love. You can't look into a thousand-year-old face and think, *I bet you were an annoying old nag.*"

"You've just put your thumb here on the print," Miss Whitfield suggested to me. As if I were six years old and playing with my father's Brownie.

I imagined myself with my hands around her throat. It came on me all of a sudden and shocked me more than the face had. I took my imaginary hands off her and gave her an imaginary and forgiving handshake instead.

In fact, I was angry with them all for refusing to believe the photograph even as they looked at it. Her face was indistinct, I grant you that. But you could see how beautiful she was. You could see the longing in those eyes. The fear. You could see she hadn't wanted to die alone, had surrounded herself with other people, but it hadn't helped her. I thought we all knew something about that, but maybe it was only me.

On payday there were forgeries to be exposed. A number of intriguing little carvings had begun to show up, all found by the same pair of brothers. The recent ones were simply too intriguing. Mallick made a show of dismissing the culprits as a lesson to the rest. It was all very good-natured. Even the brothers laughed at their exposure, left with a cheerful round of good-byes. It was, no doubt, a great disappointment to Miss Whitfield, who had been looking forward to the confrontation ever since Mallick showed us the tiny forged bear.

None of the workmen would be back until their money ran out, which meant that we would start again in two day's time with a whole new crew. Yusef, who'd found the golden goat, had been paid its weight in gold and wouldn't be back for weeks. This was a shame as he was one of our most skilled workers and a natural diplomat as well. Diplomats were always needed on our mixed crew of Armenians, Arabs, and Kurds.

The site was quiet with everyone gone. I missed the rhythmic chanting, the scraping of stone on stone, the pleasure of dim and distant laughter.

Davis and I used the day off to drive Miss Whitfield to the holy shrine of the Yezedis. Davis said that the Yezedis worship Lucifer and represent him with the symbol of the peacock. We bounced along the road, the dust so thick I had to stop every fifteen minutes and wipe down the car windows. The last few miles can only be done on foot, but by this time you've risen into the pure air and walking is a pleasure. The shrine is breathtakingly white and intricate as a wedding cake. Streams pour through descending basins in the cool courtyard and acolytes tiptoe in to bring you tea. Clearly their Lucifer is not the same as our Lucifer.

Still, we'd done our best to work Miss Whitfield up with stories of Satan worshippers so that the tranquil, restorative scene would be a nasty surprise. I figured I was getting to know what Miss Whitfield wanted. I whispered to her that the priest, whom we did not see, was said to be kept drugged so that his aunt could rule in his name; I didn't want the trip to be a complete disappointment.

Davis sat holding his small, black cup of tea in two hands and smiling sweetly. The steam from the tea clouded his spectacles. I was across from him, growing sleepy from the sun and the sound of water. Miss Whitfield had knelt by the lowest of the fountain pools. She broke the surface with her hand, so her submerged fingers seemed larger than the dry hand to which they were attached. "Tell me," Davis said to Miss Whitfield. "When you come to a place like this, even at a place like this, do you find yourself imagining a murder?"

And I thought how easy it would be to push Miss Whitfield's head under and hold it. It wasn't even a complete thought, just a flicker, really, ephemeral as the steam from Davis' tea, no emotional content, no actual desire. I put it instantly out of my mind, which was easy enough since it had hardly been there to begin with.

"Would you think I was a ghoul if I said yes?" Miss Whitfield's black hair shivered in the slight breeze. She smoothed it back with her wet fingers, dipped her hand and wet her hair again.

"I'd think you the complete professional," Davis said politely. "But it's a ghoulish profession."

"So's yours," she answered.

And then to me, "So's yours," even though I hadn't said a thing.

On our way back we stopped in town to buy bread and chocolate to add to our supper of mutton and goat cheese and wine. Davis had gotten too much sun during our outing; he was as pink as if he'd been boiled. When he came to the table he sat on a chair that wasn't solidly beneath him and fell onto the stone floor with a loud cry of alarm. I'd never seen Patwin enjoy anything so much. He could hardly chew he was laughing so hard.

Miss Whitfield was too tired to eat. Ferhid took her untouched plate back to the kitchen, where he dropped knives and slammed pot lids to communicate his disapproval until Mallick went out to mollify him.

When I was sure no one was watching, I slipped away and took three more pictures of Tu-api, moving the light between each shot. If I stared long enough through the rangefinder into the coffin, I could conjure her face just the way my photograph had recorded it, floating over her skull. If I looked directly, then the face disappeared.

When I developed the new pictures, there was no face. I took another print off my original exposure, and her face didn't show up there, either. Perhaps this should have persuaded me that the image wasn't to be trusted, was a fault of the paper and therefore unreal. But I was even more persuaded in the event, which was proving so singular and so intimate. Tu-api had shown her face only once and only to me.

"I have a bone to pick with you." Patwin caught me as I came out of the bathroom. "You're always riding me about my politics."

Patwin didn't use American idioms, so I figured he was merely repeating what some native speaker had said to him, and I figured I knew who that would be. I was outraged by the collusion, but also by the sentiment.

"You must be joking," I said. "The way you lecture me..."

"Live and let live is all I'm saying." And he brushed by without another word.

I passed Davis on the way to my bedroom. "That really hurt when I fell," he said. "I may have cracked a bone."

"I didn't laugh as hard as Patwin did," I told him.

Miss Whitfield asked us all what it was about a dig that we liked. We were sitting in the courtyard of the expedition house and only Mallick was missing, trapped in town by a heavy rain that had turned the roads to mud. The air was washed and wonderful, and the sky an ocean of cool, gray clouds. Davis and Miss Jackson were playing a game on a stone board more than four thousand years old. Four thousand years ago they would have played with colored pebbles, but they were making do with buttons. Seven such boards had been found in Tu-api's tomb, and the rules were inscribed in cuneiform though not in our dig, but back in Egypt at Carter's. This same game had been played as far away as India. Ferhid was a demon at it.

"Not the fleas," Patwin said. He was scratching at his ankles.

"Not the dust." That was Miss Jackson.

"Not the way the workmen smell," I said.

"Not the way you smell," Patwin added, all loyalty to the working class. But then, placatingly, "Not the way I smell."

"I like a routine," Davis told her. "I actually enjoy picky, painstaking work. And, of course, we're all fond of a puzzle. We all like to put things together, guess what they mean."

"I like that it's backwards." Miss Jackson won a free turn and then a second. All six of her buttons were on the board now. "You dig down from the surface and you move backwards in time as you go. Have you never wanted, desperately wanted, to go backwards in time?"

Miss Whitfield paused for a thoughtful moment. "Of course. A person might want to erase a mistake," she suggested. "Or some stupid thing said without thinking."

"I like the monotony." Patwin had his eyes closed and his face turned up to the cool sky. "Day after day after day with nothing but your own thoughts. You begin to think things that surprise you."

Davis bumped one of Miss Jackson's buttons back to the beginning. "There you go backwards in time," he said, but Miss Jackson was speaking, too, only much quieter so it took a moment to hear.

"You have to be in love with the dead," she said. She took two of her stones off the board in a single turn and bumped one of Davis'. A third stone occupied a safe square, leaving Davis no move.

He shook his fist at her, smiling. "You're a lucky woman."

"Do you know how many bodies have been found on this site alone?" Miss Jackson asked Miss Whitfield. Her voice stayed low and colorless. "Almost two thousand. Just imagine writing one of your books with two thousand dead bodies to explain. And every single one of them left someone behind, begging their gods to undo it. Bargaining. Screaming. Weeping. You can only manage a dig if you already feel so much you can't take in another thing."

A long silence followed. "Excuse me," Miss Jackson said and left the courtyard.

Miss Jackson seldom made speeches. She never, ever referred to her losses; I'd always admired that about her. I only knew about them because Patwin, who'd worked with her three seasons now, had heard it from Mallick. Patwin had hinted that she was sleeping with Mallick, but I'd seen no signs and hoped it wasn't true. Miss Jackson was not a young woman, nor a pretty one, but she was too young and too pretty for Mallick. I don't mean that Mallick's not a good guy. But honestly, few women wouldn't be.

I thought back on how she'd also told us she'd seen the face of God in the sky and how that speech, too, had been uncharacteristic. I hoped there was a simple explanation; I liked Miss Jackson and didn't want to see her handling things badly—sleeping with Mallick and rushing from a room in tears. Maybe we'd come up on some anniversary of something.

Or maybe Miss Whitfield was to blame. Miss Whitfield might make me edgy and snappish, but maybe Miss Jackson had finally melted in the sympathetic presence of another female.

"Well." The sympathetic female wrote a few words in her notebook. "I hope it wasn't something *I* said." She addressed me. "You're very quiet. Are you in love with the dead?"

Since I'd been thinking about Miss Jackson and not about myself, I had nothing prepared to say. I'm not good on the fly. "I'm not sure I do like a dig," I answered. "I'm still deciding." My heart was thudding oddly; the question had unnerved me more than it should have. So I kept talking, just to demonstrate a steadier voice. "I wanted to see some things I wouldn't see in Michigan. Mallick gave a lecture at the university and I asked some questions that he liked and he said if I could make my own way here, he could use me."

Miss Whitfield was staring at me through little eyes. From her vantage point, I could see how culpable I'd sounded, how unresponsive to the actual question. So I kept talking, which wasn't like me. "A photograph is simple. It's about the thing in the moment. I can take a picture of a dead baby and not be trying to guess why it's dead, when I'd never know if I was right. A photograph is never wrong."

She was still staring. "Rome wasn't built in a day, but every day we build Rome," I told her. I meant to use that to explain why a story was different from a photograph, but I stopped, because the longer I talked, the more suspicious she seemed. I felt unjustly accused, but also terribly, visibly guilty. "It's not a ghoulish profession," I said with as much dignity as I could find. There was a letter opener on a table by the doorway. I pictured myself picking it up and opening Miss Whitfield's throat in one clean swipe.

At that exact moment, I heard Patwin laugh, and the tension I'd been feeling vanished with the sound of it. "What?" Davis asked him. "What's so funny?"

"I was just remembering when you fell off your chair," Patwin said. He was still laughing. "How your arms flew up!"

I'd begun visiting Tu-api's tomb at night when no one would know. I'd like to say that there was nothing at all odd in this, but how defensive would that sound? I won't persuade you, so let's just skip that part.

In fact, I was disturbed by the murderous images coming over me, and the tomb seemed a quiet place to figure things out. I wasn't the sort to hurt anyone. People rarely upset or angered me. I'd never been a bully at school, didn't fight, didn't really engage much with people at all. Didn't care about anyone but myself, my mother had said once after my father died. She'd never said it again, but she hinted it. Buried it beneath the surface in every letter. Her own grief had been an awful thing to see for a six-year-old boy who'd just lost his father. If that was love, who could blame me for not wanting any part of it?

But I didn't think of myself as unengaged from the world so much as careful in it. Like many other people, I preferred watching to doing, only I preferred to do my watching within the spatial and temporal limits of the camera. A photograph is a moment you can spend your whole life looking at. I like the paradox of that.

A photograph isn't a narrative, so it's harder to impose on it. The only person who sees a photographer in a photograph is another photographer. And that's what I was doing in the privacy of the tomb. I was remembering those brief violent images of mine; I was trying to see the photographer.

They'd started up shortly after Miss Whitfield's arrival, and so they might have come from her. But they'd also begun shortly after Tu-api had shown me her face, a possibility I liked a lot less. If I remembered honestly, at the moment I'd taken Tu-api's first picture the word *murder* had been hanging in the air. The smell of smoke. The white light of the electric torches. "If you were going to murder someone," Miss Whitfield had been asking, "who would it be?"

No doubt Tu-api was herself a murderess. Patwin was always reminding me of this. The seven women in her antechamber, the groomsmen, the musician, the animals—all killed on her behalf. But I'd no wish to condemn her. In the context of those rows of dead babies, it didn't seem like much. In the history of the world, nothing at all.

What ruler in what land in what era has ever done otherwise? Name me one president, elected by and acting for us, who hasn't promised that we'll have peace just as soon as he's done killing people. Sixteen million soldiers (many of them killers themselves) dead in the Great War. Does anyone know why?

Does anyone believe we are done?

Besides, Tu-api was sorry. I'd been wrong to think that was longing in her face when it was clearly remorse. She'd wanted company in death, but that hadn't worked out. Was it possible she now wanted company in some unending world of guilt?

I found it easier to think Miss Whitfield was to blame than that Tu-api wished me ill. I'd begun to carry the print of her face in my pocket so I could pull it out and look at it whenever I was alone. I would sit on the dirt by her coffin and stare until her beautiful face floated up out of the darkness and we were, for a moment, together.

One night, walking back to my bedroom as silently as possible, I nearly collided with Mallick in the central hallway. He was wearing a nightshirt that left his saggy old knees bare. "Going to the lavatory," he explained unnecessarily, so that I knew it was true what Patwin had told me, that he'd been in the woman's wing, visiting Miss Jackson. I tried not to judge her for it, but really, what comfort could sleeping with Mallick have been?

"Me, too," I said with an equal lack of conviction.

We stood a moment, carefully not meeting each other's eyes. "So Miss Whitfield leaves tomorrow," Mallick offered finally. "She's been a lively addition." I realized then that he thought I'd been visiting Miss Whitfield. As if that wouldn't be worth your life!

A woman's face appeared in a doorway, white and sudden.

When my heart began beating again, I recognized Miss Whitfield. She didn't speak, merely noted my suspicious, nighttime rambling, my covert meeting with Mallick, and disappeared as quickly as she'd come, no doubt to write it all down before she forgot. "Taking my pictures," she called it once, as if what she did and what I did were the same, as if her imposed judgments could be compared to my dispassionate records. If I'd wanted to murder her, this would have been my last opportunity. Not that I wanted to murder her. Plus Mallick had seen me; I'd never get away with it. I went to my room and into a night of troubled dreams.

Miss Whitfield left the next morning. At Patwin's insistence, I took a group picture before she went. Patwin was always reminding me to document the work as well as the artifacts. "Take some pictures of live people today," he would say, fingering his beard with that annoying scratching sound. "Take some pictures of me."

Everyone lined up in the expedition house courtyard, staring into the morning sun. Miss Whitfield was so eager to leave that she couldn't stand still and ruined two exposures before I got one that showed her clearly. It's a formal portrait; no one is touching anyone else in our strained little arrangement of bodies.

"Was there a curse on Tu-api's tomb?" Miss Whitfield had asked us shortly after her arrival. According to the newspapers, Carter had a curse; it was one more way in which we disappointed. Though Mallick, who had his own sources, said no one could find the actual site or text of Carter's curse. Other tombs had them, so, of course, Carter couldn't be expected to do without.

The very day Carter found the entrance to Tut-ankh-Amen's tomb, a cobra ate his pet canary. "Some curse," Patwin scoffed when we read this, but Davis reminded us how canaries in mines died just to warn you death was coming for you next. And sure enough, last week, we had a telegram from Lord Wallis that Lord Carnarvon, who sponsored Carter's dig, had suddenly died in Cairo. The cause was indeterminate, but might have been a fever carried by an insect bite on his cheek. Back in England his dog had also died—this curse was most unkind to pets.

It was the dog that put Miss Whitfield over the top. She cared little for mountains of copper, gold, and ebony. She was, as Patwin had noted, being nothing but fair, no materialist. But she did love a suspicious death. She left us for Egypt just as quick as an invitation could be wrangled and transport arranged.

I believe we were all a bit disappointed to realize that none of us was to be the murderer or victim in her next book. All those murderous thoughts I'd obligingly had, all the probing we'd withstood, all the petty disputes we'd engaged in, all for nothing. The one to reap the benefit would, of course, be Carter.

We stood at the entry to the expedition house and waved. She was turned around to us, her face in the car window, smaller and smaller until it and then the car that carried her vanished entirely. "A dangerous woman," Patwin said.

"A terrible eater," said Ferhid. His tone was venomous. "A picky eater."

"I can't put my finger on exactly what it was about her," said Miss Jackson. "But there were times when she was watching us, taking notes on everything we said and did, as if she knew what we really meant and we didn't—there were times when I could have happily strangled her."

So we were all glad to see the last of her. It didn't mean she wasn't missed. It was hard to go back to how we'd been before; it was hard to stop being irritated with everyone just because she wasn't there asking us to be. There was a space left that no one else would fit inside. Ferhid kept setting her plate at the table for three days after she'd gone.

I've tried to tell all this as carefully as I could. Davis with the sunlight flashing off his spectacles. Miss Whitfield dipping her hand in the fountain. Mallick in his nightshirt. Ferhid's smile. Miss Jackson kneeling before God's face in the clouds. All that happened. All that was real. I'd rather you looked at that instead of at me. And yet here I am.

Some people are sensitive to exposure and some aren't. Miss Whitfield left her mark on me, but took no mark in return. Miss Whitfield was the sort of person who could touch Tu-api's skull, undisturbed, as it had been for centuries, and even move it and still not be changed by doing so. Me, I've always been the sensitive sort.

The night after Miss Whitfield's departure I went again to Tu-api's tomb. The silhouette of the ruined ziggurat shone in the moonlight. There was the hum of bugs; a dog barked sleepily in the distance; my footsteps thudded in the dust. The wind was cool and carried the smell of cooked chicken. My relief was enormous. The only reason I'd thought of murdering Miss Whitfield was that she was an awful woman who often talked about murder. There was nothing supernatural at work here; it was all perfectly normal, and everyone had felt the same.

The moon had risen, round as an opened rose. I walked away from it into the perfect darkness of the tomb. I owed Tu-api an apology. How could I ever have thought, even for a minute, that she'd curse me into murder? I begged for her forgiveness. It was the first time I'd spoken to her aloud.

She was not the only one listening. Gossipy Mallick had apparently told Patwin his suspicions regarding me and Miss Whitfield, and Patwin, being more discerning and trained to read puzzles far older and more mysterious than I, came upon the truth of it. He'd followed me, and when I spoke, he was the one who responded. "What's this about?" he asked, and what could I possibly say?

"You can't be coming here anymore at night by yourself." Patwin stepped toward me. "You can't be thinking this way." He took me by the arm. "Come back to bed."

I let him lead me over the moonlit dust to the expedition house. As we went, he analyzed my errors. I was guilty of romanticism, of individualism. I was guilty of ancestor worship. I had entertained the superstition of an ancient, powerful curse. I wasn't even bourgeois; I had barely made it to primitive.

There was no need to lecture me. I knew all those things. He put me to bed as if he were my mother, sitting beside me for a while, pretending nothing was wrong with me, just the way my mother had pretended. "You need a girlfriend," he suggested. "It's too bad Miss Whitfield has gone. It's too bad Miss Jackson is already spoken for."

I stopped listening. I'd just realized something about myself, something so unlikely, so unexpected, that no one would ever have guessed it. I myself would never have guessed it. Mother would never have guessed it, and she would be so surprised when she found out. The thing I realized was this: I was the sort of person who would do anything for love.

I'd never felt so joyful, so alive. Who could call that a curse? I'd never felt so serene. Mr. Davis or Mr. Patwin? Mallick or Miss Jackson or Ferhid? All or none of the above, and what if I got it wrong? But it had never been my choice to make. What I would do was whatever she asked.

Poor Patwin. I had only to turn to see his face. He'd believed so firmly in the march of history, it left him blind to the danger in the moment. Poor Miss Whitfield. Served her right, though, choosing Carter over us. How sad she'd be to have missed it all. Poor Miss Jackson. She'd never figured out that the secret is to love someone already dead. Then nothing can happen that doesn't bring the two of you closer together.

Serenity is, of course, a transitory state, just like living. Whatever Miss Jackson may wish to believe, humans being humans, eternal peace is found only in the grave and not always even there. I'm not telling you anything you don't already know.

But why spoil things with the long view? Let's leave me there in the moment, flooded with love. Patwin is talking and I am trying to make him happy by agreeing with everything he says. I agree that my infatuation with Tu-api is at an end. I agree that, circumstances being different, I would have considered Miss Jackson or even, God forbid, Miss Whitfield. I agree that when the weather grows too hot and we all go to our separate homes for the summer, I will put serious effort into finding a girlfriend who is alive. I agree that love can be usefully examined with the tool of Marxist analysis. I hand over my photograph and watch Patwin tear it up, both of us pretending there is someplace he can put those pieces where they won't last forever.

The Marianas Islands

A map of the world that does not include Utopia is not worth
even glancing at, for it leaves out the one country at which
Humanity is always landing.—Oscar Wilde

Once when I was four or five I asked my grandmother to tell me a
secret, some secret thing only grown-ups knew. She thought a moment,
then leaned down close to me and whispered. "There are no grown-
ups," she said.

According to my father, my grandmother was one of those
remarkable women who completely reinvented themselves during the
seventies. He remembers her as a sort of Betty Crocker figure. She
wore lipstick, pumps, and aprons. She put up fruits. One day she
metamorphosed into Betty Friedan. She phoned over to him in his
dorm room at college. "Mom," he said. "I've been trying to get you. I
need a shirt mended, and I need it by Friday. Can I drop it by?"

"My sewing basket is in the laundry room," she said. "Pick a
spool that matches the color of the shirt. Knot one end of the thread
and put the other end into the needle. Use the smallest needle you can
manage. I'm in jail. This is my one phone call. We've agreed to refuse
bail. You can get the needle and thread when you go by to feed Angel.
It's her night for the Tuna Platter."

Grams had joined the San Francisco Fairmont sit-in to protest racist hiring policies. She appeared on the news that night, being dragged into the police van; my dad's entire dormitory watched it. Her form, my father always said, was perfect. It was the first of many such phone calls. There was the Vietnam War. There were the nuclear tests. She chained herself to a fence in Nevada. The last wild-water rivers needed to be saved. By the time I was born, my grandmother had an arrest record the size of a Michener novel. One of my earliest memories is of my father, hanging up the phone and reaching for his coat to go and feed Angel, who was by this time an ancient Siamese with a sensitive stomach. "She won't eat if I feed her. You should see the look she gives me." My father shook his head. "'Methinks the lady doth protest too much.'"

Her husband, my grandfather, died before my father's first birthday, shot down in the Pacific, in the battle off Samar. The angriest I ever saw my grandmother was one time when my father suggested that if her husband had been alive, she might not have been quite so unrestrained. "Your father gave his life to make the world a better place," she said. "So don't you think for one minute he would have minded making his own supper in the same cause."

I, myself, at five was deeply in love with my grandmother. At sixteen, when I liked no one else, I still made an exception for her. If Grams had ruled the world, the people at my high school would have known how to treat me. You could go to her with problems; her advice was always good. She had the best possible combination of imagination and pragmatism, and she never told you you didn't have a problem when you thought you did.

I was not the only troubled person who found her serenity and sympathy irresistible. She drew a parade of eccentrics into her parlor, where they played bridge and she played straight man. When I was sixteen and had my wisdom teeth out, I was allowed to recuperate on her couch. I lay under the overhang of her enormous split-leaf philodendron, with Angel2 rumbling against my legs and a knitted afghan made in Grams' Betty Crocker days wrapped around my shoulders. Out the window the sparrows dipped and shook in the bath.

The bridge table that day included a British-Indian woman named Dot, who, for reasons of faith, ate nothing but oatmeal and black tea, and a psychic named Sam. Grams' partner was a man whose name no one knew, but who called himself the Great Unknown. Doped to the gills, I floated in and out of their conversation.

"Do you think you hear the bullet that gets you?" the Great Unknown asks as I drift away. "I mean in a battle with all the other noise. Do you think you hear the one that's all yours?" He takes a trick, gathering in the cards.

When I wake up next, Dot is dealing. This is worth waking up for. She ruffles and riffles; the cards fall in a solid sheet from one hand to the other, click satisfyingly onto the table. "But what does *normal* mean?" the Great Unknown asks, collecting and arranging his hand. "We use the word as if it means something."

Gram opens with one heart.

"I don't know anyone normal," says the Great Unknown. "Do you?"

"I know people who can pass," says Sam. "Pass."

"Three clubs," says the Great Unknown. "So our polity is based really on deception and hypocrisy. The dishonest dissemblers triumphing over the honestly deranged."

"So normal is abnormal," Dot says. "So everyone you know is normal. It's a sort of koan. Pass."

"Why in the world would you jump to three clubs?" Grams asks the Great Unknown.

"I know why," says Sam.

"Well, of course you do," Grams says to Sam. "If only you'd use your powers for good instead of evil."

A little while later I am aware of Grams shuffling. "I don't care if they want to hang suspended by their feet in gas masks and scuba gear," she says. "In fact, I admire their imagination. I just don't see why they insist on calling it sex."

I wake up next in tears. The air has the early tint of evening, Angel is gone, and my mouth is full of blood. Up until now, the extractions have been good fun—sleep, and dreams, and narcotics. But the anesthetic is wearing off. There is a *pop, pop, pop* of pain pulsing in my jaw, and my mouth tastes of the ocean.

"Do you think you could eat something?" Grams asks, giving me a large pill and a glass of warmish water to chase it down.

"No." I am really crying now. "This is awful." My speech is muffled. I realize I have layers of gauze shoved into the back of my mouth. I pull them out and they are soaked red and smell of sickness.

Dot and Sam and the Great Unknown crowd around my couch. It's the final scene in *The Wizard of Oz.* "Don't cry," says Dot. "We can't bear it." She strokes my hand open, traces along the lines with a fingernail. "Very good," she assures me. "Very deep, distinctive lines. Very little confusion in your life."

"I suppose that's good," the Great Unknown says doubtfully. "Do you really believe in palmistry?" The Great Unknown prides himself on hardheaded skepticism.

"I trained in India," says Dot.

While Dot is reading my palm, Sam is reading my mind. "Mind over matter," he suggests, and then recoils, presumably from what I think of his suggestion.

I am in such pain, it makes me want to be rude. "I don't believe in palmistry or ESP. I'm so sorry." I am, of course, no such thing, and Sam knows it.

"If I was Tinkerbell, you'd be sorry," says Sam. "Real sorry." He clears his throat two or three times. "I sense that I'm developing a cough."

"Here's what I don't believe in," says the Great Unknown. He ticks them off on his fingers for me. "I don't believe in astrology, numerology, pyramid power. I don't believe in the tooth fairy, sad for you, because you stand to make out well today. I don't believe in God, although I accord him the capital G, as a courtesy to those who do." He pauses here to nod to Grams, who has always been a churchgoer, then picks right up. "I don't believe in phlogiston, extraterrestrials who abduct you and probe Uranus, the organ box, Silva Mind Control, Scientology"—he has come to the end of his fingers and starts with the first one again—"or witchcraft."

"Abracadabra," says Grams, and pulls a red bandanna out of her sleeve for me. I wipe my eyes and blow my nose. The bandanna smells of Grams and her Estee Lauder cologne.

"I think that our inept government could never keep a secret as big as a CIA-slash-Mafia-slash-Cuban conspiracy to kill JFK," says the Great Unknown. "Or fake the Moon Landing, although I could be wrong about that one—that one might not be too hard.

"What I do believe in is the desperate fight against the perils of routine living that they all represent. I believe in each man's need to feel that he has somehow been chosen. It's not everyone who has a submarine." He fixes Grams with a stern look. "The rest of us must simply make do with Elvis sightings.

"Life is a series of evasive maneuvers," he observes in conclusion. "You have to envy anyone with the means to make a clean escape."

"But I could never do that," says Grams. "I could never leave the rest of you behind."

—ɯ—

Karen Joy Fowler

Perhaps it is a little late to be bringing up the submarine. Not quite cricket, not exactly Chekhovian of me. There is no doubt that the submarine looms very large in my family lore. It was designed and built by my great-grandfather—not my grandmother's father, but her husband's. In my defense, let me just add that it's really a very small submarine, very unimposing, a one-person affair, no more than fourteen feet long.

And it's not as if the submarine were on the mantelpiece. No, sadly, the submarine lies sunk in the furry scum of Lake Emily. Lake Emily is a small body of water, a pond, really, with an oily surface and no fish more interesting than perch. It occupies the northwest corner of the Gutierrez property about fifty miles north of my grandmother's house.

For the longest time the submarine was in my grandmother's garage. I've been inside it often, and it's not all that thrilling. It had a stale, metallic smell. Here is my objection to submarines and space travel: not enough windows. What difference does it make if you're in outer space, or underwater, or wherever, if you can't feel, or hear, or see, or smell it? You might as well be locked in a closet. But my grandmother tells me it's too dark to see under the water anyway. "The fall is the lovely part," she says. "The water goes from blue to gray to black, as if you're out in space, falling through the stars."

Maria Gutierrez and the Great Unknown took the sub out one day to see how hard she would be to handle, and, having forgotten to tighten two screws in the bottom, filled her up immediately with water and ran her aground. They learned a lot in the process, however, and the Great Unknown was all for hoisting her up, drying her out, and taking her straight to Scotland. Grams was not opposed to this project, but she had been working with the World Hunger people, and cranes and divers would have to be organized, and she hadn't gotten around to it. Besides, she wanted the Great Unknown to work out for a while first. She was not sure he was physically fit enough. Like her, he was in his sixties. We thought. The submarine was built for a younger man.

Although my great-grandfather spent the latter half of his life convinced he was being stalked by the Fenians, it was a point of honor in my family to consider him a genius. The party line was that he was one of those nineteenth-century men who were masters of many fields, sort of like the explorer Richard Burton. Genius and madness have a particular affinity for each other, my father says, which doesn't mean that there's not a whole lot of madness and only modest amounts of genius in the world. My great-grandfather had little formal education, but a wonderfully prehensile mind. He was a tolerable musician, a decent artist in the pen-drawing school, and spectacularly good with gadgets. One day, no one remembers why, he played the violin for eight straight hours. In doing this, he strained a nerve in his left hand from which it took him some weeks to recover. This lack of music brought about a period of frustration and general twitchiness that just about drove his wife crazy. "Go take a walk," she told him. "Learn to ride a bicycle."

The bicycle is a wonderfully designed machine. My great-grand-father had been enchanted with them from the very start. Riding them was a different matter. He came back with a sprained ankle and had to be put to bed. The situation reached crisis proportions.

But one morning, when his wife took him his breakfast, she found him calm and clear-eyed, scribbling away on the inside covers of several books. "Are you aware that most of the world is underwater?" he asked her. "What mountains we have never climbed. What caves we have never explored. What jungles!" The year was 1910. My great-grandfather had suddenly noticed that women were about to get the vote. When that happened, he believed, they would embark on a devastating national shopping spree. In anticipation, he was looking to get out of paying his taxes. The first tax-time after women got the vote he planned to spend safely underwater.

The big surprise was that he actually built her. He started with a thirty-inch model he could maneuver through the rain barrel. It was propelled by a spring and the insides of a pocket watch. The fourteen-foot version used a bicycle chain and pedals. Pitch and direction were controlled by levers in the nose. These were adjusted by hand. To propel the boat took all four limbs. It took strength and coordination. It took practice. She was merely a prototype. My great-grandfather was a family man; the final submarine was supposed to be large enough to hold his wife and son. This early model he called the *New Day*, in honor of Day, the tragic inventor of an early sub.

Day's version was much like an ordinary boat, only it had an airtight chamber inside. Day occupied the chamber and then his associates sank the boat by piling more than thirty tons of stones on it. It worked like a dream. But the same associates were less zealous in raising the craft. Day was sealed tight in his chamber and could only be brought up by removing the stones, which were now under several yards of water. This required divers and continuous effort. Somehow, there was a miscommunication between the associates. Each thought the other was organizing the ascent; each had private and pressing business elsewhere. Day was never recovered. It was a story and name that made my great-grandmother very nervous.

Great-grandfather worked with the *New Day* every weekend in the Passaic River. He grounded her three times before he made the crossing. The locals began to plan picnics with roast corn and sack races around his field trials. He would emerge from the craft to cheers and toasts. It was, undoubtedly, a happy time for him. But at the end of the last trial run, he told his wife he had seen a man watching him with binoculars from behind a tree. He came home upset, agitated. A week later, the *New Day* disappeared. "So the Fenians have her at last," he said calmly. "And a very bad day indeed to the man who tries her out."

Another week passed, and then he disappeared himself. Because of the timing, his family believed that his talk of losing the submarine had been a ruse, and that he had finally taken the *New Day* down. "Those underwater mountains," Grams told me her mother-in-law said to her once, years later. "You'd have to climb them downwards." It was the sort of thing you might say if you'd given it a whole lot of thought. She waited a long time for him to surface.

I'll tell you what I think. A submarine can't have been cheap and he had a fiddler's salary. Where did he get the money to build the *New Day?* No one in the family knows, but it's my belief that the paranoid delusions which began to haunt him were neither paranoid nor delusionary. "Went over the edge" was the way the family finally chose to explain it, but "sleeps with the fishes" is the phrase that comes to my mind.

Years later, after he was declared dead, and his wife had also died, and also his son, my grandmother received a letter from an attorney. His client was a man in upstate New York, one James Fortis, who had known my great-grandfather. One night my great-grandfather had come to him and asked that he hide the *New Day* in his barn, to prevent her, he said, from falling into the wrong hands. He made Mr. Fortis swear never to speak of it, since those who wanted the boat were cunning, relentless, and well connected. He would be back for her soon, my great-grandfather had said, and had gone in a hurry, looking right and left.

Out of friendship, Mr. Fortis had agreed, and had kept the secret, although the years dragged on and the space taken up by the submarine, according to the letter, could have held four additional cows. But now Mr. Fortis was an elderly man with medical expenses. He was selling the farm, and he wished to be rid of the submarine.

Karen Joy Fowler

His attorney had determined that the sub belonged to Grams. Included in the letter was a bill for thirty-five years of storage. In addition, the sub had to be shipped all the way across the country. It took a chunk of change.

Grams moved her car out of the garage and the submarine in. "A person with a submarine will never lack for friends," she was fond of telling me, and, of course, someday the submarine was to be mine.

I wonder sometimes about my grandmother as a young woman, and when I think it through, the Betty Crocker stuff seems just as remarkable as the Betty Friedan. She was a war widow with a young child. That Betty Crocker my father remembers, she must have been made with guilt, smoke, and mirrors. Grams never remarried, although even in her sixties there were opportunities. I see now that my grandmother must have spent her whole life desperately in love with a dead man.

One of the times I asked about my grandfather, Grams showed me a map. It was made of nylon, mostly white, but printed with a grid and a number of curving red arrows. Along the base of the grid were the words *Map of the Marianas Islands.* And if you looked closely, you might actually be able to find the islands, green flea specks in the enormous expanse of white ocean.

So it was, in fact, a map of air and water. It had been commissioned by the War Department, which gave it to pilots during the war in the Pacific. The theory was that if a pilot was shot down, he could calculate his last known position, catch the nearest current, and float to land. The War Department, having the same map, would know where to look for him. It gave me a sense of vertigo, trying to imagine what it would be like, falling into that featureless landscape with nothing to secure you but that featureless map.

At the time of my extractions, while I lay on her couch and wrapped myself into her afghan, and a phantom bird pecked rhythmically into the sorest part of my jaw, Grams was already suffering from the first signs of Alzheimer's. I don't know if she knew this; certainly she was far too cunning to be caught at it. Three years later it was unmistakable. She got lost on the way to the corner market, and she couldn't remember my mother's name. "Eleanor," Dad reminded her. "Ellie. Why did you always tell people Ellie was much too good for me?" Growing up as he did, with only the two of them, many things were tangled between them. He was hastily trying to settle what he could in those lucid moments before she disappeared.

"I was being charmingly modest," she said.

I was off at college now and paying little attention. She moved in with my parents for a while, and then Dad called to tell me Grams had gone into a home. Not only did this move break her heart, it also emptied her bank accounts. Her house would have to be sold. Angel2 was staying on with my father and mother and was no happier about it than Grams. It was a short phone call with a number of silences.

The next time I talked to my father he seemed better. "They've prescribed a pill for paranoia," he told me. "But she's too suspicious to take it." The nurses were in an uproar. My father was obviously charmed.

By the time I got to see her it was Christmas break. I'd come home, and Dad and I had gone over together. By now she was taking her medications. "She's being a good girl today," the nurse told us. "She's being an angel."

Grams was wearing a robe printed with little yellow flowers although she had never been a little-yellow-flower kind of person. Her hair stuck out around her ears as if no one had brushed it. I gave her a box of chocolate turtles to which she was indifferent. She didn't seem to know I was there. Perhaps I was not the person she loved best in the world, after all. I was content at this time to give up the honor to my father. "How are you?" Grams asked him.

"I'm good."

"And how are your father and mother?"

"My father's fine," said Dad. "But we're a little worried about Mom."

The whole time we were there, we could hear another woman down the hall. "Help me, please. Help me, please," she sobbed in a continuous rhythmical plea.

"That goes on all the time," my father told me. "Like she was frozen in some moment of torment." His eyes were cracked with red, and glassy. "At least that's not Mom." When we got back in the car to drive home, he mentioned the sobbing woman again. "I just keep thinking, what if it's something simple? What if she just needs her socks pulled up or a glass of water or something? What if it was something we could fix, but she's forgotten how to say it?"

My father had joined the Food Not Bombs people. When we went back to the house, there were stacks of pamphlets in the living room. Angel2 lay in the sunshine on top of one and raised her head crossly at the disturbance. "Now we see the real danger of this three-strikes nonsense," my father said. "Now that they want to make it a felony to feed people." He pitched his voice to match that of the Wicked Witch of the West. "What a world, what a world."

The Great Unknown had also gone to the nursing home to visit with my grandmother, and afterward he dropped by the house to see me as well. He was calling himself Carroll Leary now. "Where's the submarine?" he asked me, almost immediately, so I was cautious when I answered; it occurred to me that Leary was an Irish name and that Carroll had always been extremely interested in the *New Day*. It would be so like Grams to play bridge with the IRA. I just said she was in storage, and that she was mine now.

In fact, she was right where he left her, back in the mud on the floor of Lake Emily. Grams was able to keep her, because she was a hidden asset, and she's mine, all right, any time I can raise the money to raise her. "I hope you handle it as gracefully as your grandmother always did. She didn't choose it, you know. She married into it," said Carroll. He gave me a look. Don't ask me what kind of look. I could never read him. "It's an enormous responsibility, owning a submarine," he said.

My father joined us. "It's an enormous lack of responsibility," he argued. "When you have a boat, you don't need a plan"—but I know what my grandmother would want. Someday I'll hoist her up, take her down, join Greenpeace. When I get older, say around menopause, I'll become a pirate, harry the shipping lanes along the coast. When I'm really old, I'll settle in the Marianas Islands.

That night I slept again in my old bedroom in my parents' house. I hadn't been there for a while, and I woke once during the night, completely disoriented. It was so dark, even though I'd been sleeping, even though my night vision was fully engaged, I couldn't see. The first thing you need to know is where you are. I had to imagine shapes around me; I had to make up a context. I closed my eyes and went on imagining. I made myself hear voices around me, hushed so as not to wake me, and hands stroking my hair, straightening my blankets. The bed began to rock, like a boat, like a cradle. Then I got lucky; I was home. I fell asleep again, and it was a slow, sweet descent.

Halfway People

Thunder, wind, and waves. You in your cradle. You've never heard these noises before, and they are making you cry.

Here, child. Let me wrap you in a blanket and my arms, take you to the big chair by the fire, and tell you a story. My father's too old and deaf to hear and you too young to understand. If you were older or he younger, I couldn't tell it, this story so dangerous that tomorrow I must forget it entirely and make up another.

But a story never told is also a danger, particularly to the people in it. So here, tonight, while I remember.

It starts with a girl named Maura, which is my name, too.

In the winter, Maura lives by the sea. In the summer, she doesn't. In the summer, she and her father rent two shabby rooms inland and she walks every morning to the coast, where she spends the day washing and changing bedding, sweeping the sand off the floors, scouring and dusting. She does this for many summer visitors, including the ones who live in her house. Her father works at a big hotel on the point. He wears a blue uniform, opens the heavy front door for guests and closes it behind them. At night, Maura and her father walk on tired feet back to their rooms. Sometimes it's hard for Maura to remember that this was ever different.

But when she was little, she lived by the sea in all seasons. It was a lonely coast then, a place of rocky cliffs, forests, wild winds, and beaches of coarse sand. Maura could play from morning to night and never see another person, only gulls and dolphins and seals. Her father was a fisherman.

Then a doctor who lived in the capital began to recommend the sea air to his wealthy patients. A businessman built the hotel and shipped in finer sand. Pleasure boats with colored sails filled the fishing berths. The coast became fashionable, though nothing could be done about the winds.

One day the landlord came to tell Maura's father that he'd rented out their home to a wealthy friend. It was just for two weeks and for so much money, he could only say yes. The landlord said it would happen this once, and they could move right back when the two weeks were over.

But the next year he took it for the entire summer and then for every summer after that. The winter rent was also raised.

Maura's mother was still alive then. Maura's mother loved their house by the ocean. The inland summers made her pale and thin. She sat for hours at the window watching the sky for the southward migrations, the turn of the season. Sometimes she cried and couldn't say why.

Even when winter came, she was unhappy. She felt the lingering presence of the summer guests, their sorrows and troubles as chilled spaces she passed through in the halls and doorways. When she sat in her chair, the back of her neck was always cold; her fingers fretted and she couldn't stay still.

But Maura liked the bits of clues the summer people left behind—a strange spoon in a drawer, a half-eaten jar of jam on a shelf, the ashes of papers in the fireplace. She made up stories from them of different lives in different places. Lives worthy of stories.

The summer people brought gossip from the court and tales from even farther away. A woman had grown a pumpkin as big as a carriage in her garden, hollowed it out, and slept there, which for some reason couldn't be allowed so now there was a law against sleeping in pumpkins. A new country had been found where the people had hair all over their bodies and ran about on their hands and feet like dogs, but were very musical. A child had been born in the east who could look at anyone and know how they would die, which frightened his neighbors so much, they'd killed him, as he'd always known they would. A new island had risen in the south, made of something too solid to be water and too liquid to be earth. The king had a son.

The summer Maura turned nine years old, her mother was all bone and eyes and bloody coughing. One night, her mother came to her bed and kissed her. "Keep warm," she whispered, in a voice so soft Maura was never certain she hadn't dreamed it. Then Maura's mother walked from the boarding house in her nightgown and was never seen again. Now it was Maura's father who grew thin and pale.

One year later, he returned from the beach in great excitement. He'd heard her mother's voice in the surf. She'd said she was happy now, repeated it in every wave. He began to tell Maura bedtime stories in which her mother lived in underwater palaces and ate off golden clamshells. Sometimes in these stories her mother was a fish. Sometimes a seal. Sometimes a woman. He watched Maura closely for signs of her mother's afflictions. But Maura was her father's daughter, able to travel in her mind and stay put in her body.

Years passed. One summer day, a group of young men arrived while Maura was still cleaning the seaside house. They stepped into the kitchen, threw their bags onto the floor, and raced each other down to the water. Maura didn't know that one had stayed behind until he spoke. "Which is your room?" he asked her. He had hair the color of sand.

She took him to her bedroom with its whitewashed walls, feather-filled pillows, window of buckled glass. He put his arms around her, breath in her ear. "I'll be in your bed tonight," he said. And then he released her and she left, her blood passing though her veins so quickly, she was never sure which she had wanted more, to be held or let go.

More years. The capital became a place where books and heretics were burned. The king died and his son became king, but he was a young king and it was really the archbishop who ruled. The pleasure-loving summer people said little about this or anything else. Even on the coast, they feared the archbishop's spies.

A man Maura might have married wed a summer girl instead. Maura's father grew old and hard of hearing, though if you looked him straight in the face when you spoke, he understood you well enough. If Maura minded seeing her former suitor walking along the cliffs with his wife and children, if her father minded no longer being able to hear her mother's voice in the waves, they never said so to each other.

The hotel had let her father go at the end of the last summer. They were very sorry, they told Maura, since he'd worked there so long. But guests had been complaining that they had to shout to make him hear, and he seemed with age to have sunk into a general confusion. Addled, they said.

Without his earnings, Maura and her father wouldn't make the winter rent. They had this one more winter and then would never live by the sea again. It was another thing they didn't say to each other. Possibly her father didn't know.

One morning, Maura realized that she was older than her mother had been on the night she'd disappeared. She realized that it had been many years since anyone had wondered aloud in her presence why such a pretty young girl wasn't married.

To shake off the sadness of these thoughts, she went for a walk along the cliffs. The wind was bitter and whipped the ends of her hair against her cheeks so hard they stung. She was about to go back, when she saw a man wrapped in a great black cape. He stood without moving, staring down at the water and the rocks. He was so close to the cliff edge, Maura was afraid he meant to jump.

There now, child. This is the wrong time to go to sleep. Maura is about to fall in love.

Maura walked toward the man, carefully so as not to startle him. She reached out to touch him, then took hold of his arm through the thick cape. He didn't respond. When she turned him from the cliff, his eyes were empty, his face like glass. He was younger than she'd thought. He was many years younger than she.

"Come away from the edge," she told him, and still he gave no sign of hearing, but allowed himself to be led, step by slow step, back to the house.

"Where did he come from?" her father asked. "How long will he stay? What is his name?" and then turned to address those same questions to the man himself. There was no answer.

Maura took the man's cape from him. One of his arms was an arm. The other was a wing of white feathers.

Someday, little one, you'll come to me with a wounded bird. It can't fly, you'll say, because it's too little or someone threw a stone or a cat mauled it. We'll bring it inside and put it in a warm corner, make a nest of old towels. We'll feed it with our hands and protect it, if we can, if it lives, until it's strong enough to leave us. As we do this, you'll be thinking of the bird, but I'll be thinking of how Maura once did all those things for a wounded man with a single wing.

Her father went to his room. Soon Maura heard him snoring. She made the young man tea and a bed by the fire. That first night, he couldn't stop shaking. He shook so hard Maura could hear his upper teeth banging against his lower. He shivered and sweated until she lay down beside him, put her arms about him, and calmed him with stories, some of them true, about her mother, her life, the people who'd stayed in this house and drowsed through summer mornings in this room.

She felt the tension leave his body. As he slept, he turned onto his side, curled against her. His wing spread across her shoulder, her breasts. She listened all night, sometimes awake and sometimes in dreams, to his breathing. No woman in the world could sleep a night under that wing and not wake up in love.

He recovered slowly from his fevers and sweats. When he was strong enough, he found ways to make himself useful, though he seemed to know nothing about those tasks that keep a house running. One of the panes in the kitchen window had slipped its channel. If the wind blew east off the ocean, the kitchen smelled of salt and sang like a bell. Maura's father couldn't hear it, so he hadn't fixed it. Maura showed the young man how to true it up, his one hand soft between her two.

Soon her father had forgotten how recently he'd arrived and began to call him *my son* and *your brother*. His name, he told Maura, was Sewell. "I wanted to call him Dillon," her father said. "But your mother insisted on Sewell."

Sewell remembered nothing of his life before, believing himself to be, as he'd been told, the old man's son. He had such beautiful manners. He made Maura feel cared for, attended to in a way she'd never been before. He treated her with all the tenderness a boy could give his sister. Maura told herself it was enough.

She worried about the summer that was coming. Sewell fit into their winter life. She saw no place for him in summer. She was outside, putting laundry on the line, when a shadow passed over her, a great flock of white birds headed toward the sea. She heard them calling, the low-pitched, sonorous sound of horns. Sewell ran from the house, his face turned up, his wing open and beating like a heart. He remained there until the birds had vanished over the water. Then he turned to Maura. She saw his eyes and knew that he'd come back into himself. She could see it was a sorrowful place to be.

But he said nothing and neither did she, until that night, after her father had gone to bed. "What's your name?" she asked.

He was silent awhile. "You've both been so kind to me," he said finally. "I never imagined such kindness at the hands of strangers. I'd like to keep the name you gave me."

"Can the spell be broken?" Maura asked then, and he looked at her in confusion. She gestured to his wing.

"This?" he said, raising it. "This *is* the spell broken."

A log in the fire collapsed with a sound like a hiss. "You've heard of the king's marriage? To the witch-queen?" he asked.

Maura knew only that the king had married.

"It happened this way," he said, and told her how his sister had woven shirts of nettles and how the archbishop had accused her of witchcraft, and the people sent her to the fire. How the king, her husband, said he loved her, but did nothing to save her, and it was her brothers, all of them swans, who encircled her until she broke the spell, and they were men again, all except for his single wing.

So now she was wife to a king who would have let her burn, and queen of those who'd sent her to the fire. These were her people, this her life. There was little in it that he'd call love. "My brothers don't mind the way I do," he said. "They're not as close to her. We were the youngest together, she and I."

He said that his brothers had settled easily enough into life at court. He was the only one whose heart remained divided. "A halfway heart, unhappy to stay, unhappy to go," he said, "a heart like your mother's." This took Maura by surprise. She'd thought he'd slept through her stories about her mother. Her breath grew thin and quick. He must also remember then how she'd slept beside him.

He said that in his dreams, he still flew. It hurt to wake in the morning, find himself with nothing but his clumsy feet. And at the change of seasons, the longing to be in the air, to be on the move, was so intense, it overtook him. Maybe that was because the curse had never been completely lifted. Maybe it was because of the wing.

"You won't be staying then," Maura said. She said this carefully, no shaking in her voice. Staying in the house by the sea had long been the thing Maura most wanted. She would still have a mother if they'd only been able to stay in the house by the sea.

"There's a woman I've loved all my life," he answered. "We quarreled when I left; I can't leave it like that. We don't choose whom we love," he told Maura, so gently that she knew he knew. If she wasn't to be loved in return, she would have liked not to be pitied for it. She got neither of these wishes. "But people have this advantage over swans, to put their unwise loves aside and love another. Not me. I'm too much swan for that."

He left the next morning. "Good-bye, father," he said, kissing the old man. "I'm off to find my fortune." He kissed Maura. "Thanks for your kindness and your stories. You've the gift of contentment," he said, and as soon as he named it, he took it from her.

We come now to the final act. Keep your eyes shut tight, little one. The fire inside is dying and the wind outside. As I rock you, monsters are moving in the deep.

Maura's heart froze in her chest. Summertime came and she said good-bye to the seaside house and felt nothing. The landlord had sold it. He went straight to the bars to drink to his good fortune. "For more than it's worth," he told everyone, a few cups in. "Triple its worth," a few cups later.

The new owners took possession in the night. They kept to themselves, which made the curious locals more curious. A family of men, the baker told Maura. He'd seen them down at the docks. They asked more questions than they'd answer. They were looking for sailors off a ship called the *Faucon Dieu*. No one knew why they'd come or how long they'd stay, but they had the seaside house guarded as if it were a fort. Or a prison. You couldn't take the road past without one or another of them stopping you.

Gossip arrived from the capital—the queen's youngest brother had been banished, and the queen, who loved him, was sick from it. She'd been sent into seclusion until her health and spirits returned. Maura overheard this in a kitchen as she was cleaning. There was more, but the sound of the ocean had filled Maura's ears and she couldn't hear the rest. Her heart shivered and her hands shook.

That night she couldn't sleep. She got up, and like her mother before her, walked out the door in her nightgown. She walked the long distance to the sea, skirting the seaside house. The moonlight was a road on the water. She could imagine walking on it as, perhaps, her mother had done. Instead she climbed to the cliff where she'd first seen Sewell. And there he stood again, just as she remembered, wrapped in his cape. She called to him, her breath catching so his name was a stutter. The man in the cape turned, and he resembled Sewell strongly, but he had two arms and all of Maura's years. "I'm sorry," she said. "I thought you were someone else."

"Is it Maura?" he asked, and the voice was very like Sewell's voice. He walked toward her. "I meant to call on you," he said, "to thank you for your kindness to my brother."

The night wasn't cold, but Maura's nightgown was thin. The man took off his cape, put it around her shoulders as if she were a princess.

Karen Joy Fowler

It had been a long time since a man had treated her with such care. Sewell had been the last. But Sewell had been wrong about one thing. She would never trade her unwise love for another, even if offered by someone with Sewell's same gentleness and sorrow. "Is he here?" Maura asked.

He'd been exiled, the man said, and the penalty for helping him was death. But they'd had warning. He'd run for the coast, with the archbishop's men hard behind him, to a foreign ship where his brothers had arranged passage only hours before it became illegal to do so. The ship was to take him across the sea to the country where they'd lived as children. He was to send a pigeon to let them know he'd arrived, but no pigeon had come. "My sister, the queen," the man said, "has suffered from the not-knowing. We all have."

Then, just yesterday, for the price of a whiskey, a middle brother had gotten a story from a sailor at the docks. It was a story the sailor had heard recently in another harbor, not a story he'd lived. There was no way to know how much of it was true.

In this story there was a ship whose name the sailor didn't remember, becalmed in a sea he couldn't name. The food ran out and the crew lost their wits. There was a passenger on this ship, a man with a deformity, a wing where his arm should be. The crew decided he was the cause of their misfortunes. They'd seized him from his bed, dragged him up on deck, taken bets on how long he'd stay afloat. "Fly away," they told him as they threw him overboard. "Fly away, little bird."

And he did.

As he fell, his arm had become a second wing. For just one moment he'd been an angel. And then a moment later, a swan. He'd circled the ship three times and vanished into the horizon. "My brother had seen the face of the mob before," the man said, "and it made him regret being human. If he's a swan again, he's glad."

Maura closed her eyes. She pushed the picture of Sewell the angel, Sewell the swan, away, made him a tiny figure in the distant sky. "Why was he exiled?" she asked.

"An unnatural intimacy with the queen. No proof, mind you. The king is a good man, but the archbishop calls the tune. And he's always hated our poor sister. Eager to believe the most vile gossip," said the man. "Our poor sister. Queen of a people who would have burned her and warmed their hands at the fire. Married to a man who'd let them."

"He said you didn't mind that," Maura told him.

"He was wrong."

The man walked Maura back to her rooms, his cape still around her. He said he'd see her again, but summer ended and winter came with no word. The weather turned bitter. Maura was bitter, too. She could taste her bitterness in the food she ate, the air she breathed.

Her father couldn't understand why they were still in their rented rooms. "Do we go home today?" he asked every morning and often more than once. September became October. November became December. January became February.

Then late one night, Sewell's brother knocked at Maura's window. It was iced shut; she heard a crack when she forced it open. "We leave in the morning," the man said. "I'm here to say good-bye. And to beg you and your father to go to the house as soon as you wake tomorrow, without speaking to anyone. We thank you for the use of it, but it was always yours."

He was gone before Maura could find the thing that she should say; thank you or good-bye or please don't go.

In the morning, she and her father did as directed. The coast was wrapped in a fog that grew thicker the farther they walked. As they neared the house, they saw shadows, the shapes of men in the mist. Ten men, clustered together around a smaller, slighter figure. The eldest brother waved Maura past him toward the house. Her father went to speak to him. Maura went inside.

Sometimes summer guests left cups and sometimes hairpins. These guests had left a letter, a cradle, and a baby.

The letter said: *My brother told me you could be trusted with this child. I give him to you. My brother told me you would make up a story explaining how you've come to own this house and have this child, a story so good that people would believe it. This child's life depends on you doing so. No one must ever know he exists. The truth is a danger none of us would survive.*

"Burn this letter," is how it ended. There was no signature. The writing was a woman's.

Maura lifted the baby. She loosened the blanket in which he was wrapped. A boy. Two arms. Ten fingers. She wrapped him up again, rested her cheek on the curve of his scalp. He smelled of soap. And very faintly, beneath that, Maura smelled the sea. "This child will stay put," Maura said aloud, as if she had the power to cast such a spell.

No child should have a mother with a frozen heart. Maura's cracked and opened. All the love that she would someday have for this child was already there, inside her heart, waiting for him. But she couldn't feel one thing and not another. She found herself weeping, half joyful, half undone with grief. Good-bye to her mother in her castle underwater. Good-bye to the summer life of drudgery and rented rooms. Good-bye to Sewell in his castle in the air.

Her father came into the house. "They gave me money," he said wonderingly. His arms were full. Ten leather pouches. "So much money."

When you've heard more of the old stories, little one, you'll see that the usual return on a kindness to a stranger is three wishes. The usual wishes are for a fine house, fortune, and love. Maura was where she'd never thought to be, at the very center of one of the old stories, with a prince in her arms.

"Oh!" Her father saw the baby. He reached out, and the pouches of money spilled to the floor. He stepped on them without noticing. "Oh!" He took the swaddled child from her. He, too, was crying. "I dreamed that Sewell was a grown man and left us," he said. "But now I wake and he's a baby. How wonderful to be at the beginning of his life with us instead of the end. Maura! How wonderful life is."

Standing Room Only

for John Kessel

On Good Friday 1865, Washington, D.C., was crowded with tourists and revelers. Even the Willard, which claimed to be the largest hotel in the country, with room for 1200 guests, had been booked to capacity. Its lobbies and sitting rooms were hot with bodies. Gas light hissed from golden chandeliers, spilled over the doormen's uniforms of black and maroon. Many of the revelers were women. In 1865, women were admired for their stoutness and went anywhere they could fit their hoop skirts. The women at the Willard wore garishly colored dresses with enormous skirts and resembled great inverted tulips. The men were in swallow coats.

Outside it was almost spring. The forsythia bloomed, dusting the city with yellow. Weeds leapt up in the public parks; the roads melted to mud. Pigs roamed like dogs about the city, and dead cats by the dozens floated in the sewers and perfumed the rooms of the White House itself.

The Metropolitan Hotel contained an especially rowdy group of celebrants from Baltimore, who passed the night of April 13 toasting everything under the sun. They resurrected on the morning of the fourteenth, pale and spent, surrounded by broken glass and sporting bruises they couldn't remember getting.

It was the last day of Lent. The war was officially over, except for

Joseph Johnston's confederate army and some action out West. The citizens of Washington, D.C., still began each morning reading the daily death list. If anything, this task had taken on an added urgency. To lose someone you loved now, with the rest of the city madly, if grimly, celebrating, would be unendurable.

The guests in Mary Surratt's boarding house began the day with a breakfast of steak, eggs and ham, oysters, grits, and whiskey. Mary's seventeen-year old daughter, Anna, was in love with John Wilkes Booth. She had a picture of him hidden in the sitting room, behind a lithograph entitled "Morning, Noon, and Night." She helped her mother clear the table, and she noticed with a sharp and unreasonable disapproval that one of the two new boarders, one of the men who only last night had been given a room, was staring at her mother.

Mary Surratt was neither a pretty women, nor a clever one, nor was she young. Anna was too much of a romantic, too star and stage-struck, to approve. It was one thing to lie awake at night in her attic bedroom, thinking of JW. It was another to imagine her mother playing any part in such feelings.

Anna's brother John once told her that five years ago a woman named Henrietta Irving had tried to stab Booth with a knife. Failing, she'd thrust the blade into her own chest instead. He seemed to be under the impression that this story would bring Anna to her senses. It had, as anyone could have predicted, the opposite effect. Anna had also heard rumors that Booth kept a woman in a house of prostitution near the White House. And once she had seen a piece of paper on which Booth had been composing a poem. You could make out the final version:

Now, in this hour, that we part,
I will ask to be forgotten, *never*

But, in thy pure and guileless heart,
Consider me thy friend, dear Eva.

Anna would sit in the parlor while her mother dozed and pretend she was the first of these women, and if she tired of that, she would sometimes dare to pretend she was the second, but most often she liked to imagine herself the third.

Flirtations were common and serious, and the women in Washington worked hard at them. A war in the distance always provides a rich context of desperation, while at the same time granting women a bit of extra freedom. They might quite enjoy it, if the price they paid were anything but their sons.

The new men had hardly touched their food, cutting away the fatty parts of the meat and leaving them in a glistening greasy wasteful pile. They'd finished the whiskey, but made faces while they drank. Anna had resented the compliment of their eyes and, paradoxically, now resented the insult of their plates. Her mother set a good table.

In fact, Anna did not like them and hoped they would not be staying. She had often seen men outside the Surratt Boarding House lately, men who busied themselves in unpersuasive activities when she passed them. She connected these new men to those, and she was perspicacious enough to blame their boarder Louis Wiechmann, for the lot of them, without ever knowing the extent to which she was right. She had lived for the past year in a Confederate household in the heart of Washington. Everyone around her had secrets. She had grown quite used to this.

Wiechmann was a permanent guest at the Surratt Boarding House, He was a fat, friendly man who worked in the office of the Commissary General of Prisons and shared John Surratt's bedroom. Secrets were what Wiechmann traded in. He provided John, who was a courier for the Confederacy, with substance for his covert messages south. But then Wiechmann had also, on a whim, sometime in March, told the clerks in the office that a Secesh plot was being hatched against the president in the very house where he roomed.

It created more interest than he had anticipated. He was called into the office of Captain McDavitt and interviewed at length. As a result, the Surratt boarding house was under surveillance from March through April, although it is an odd fact that no records of the surveillance or the interview could be found later.

Anna would surely have enjoyed knowing this. She liked attention as much as most young girls. And this was the backdrop of a romance. Instead, all she could see was that something was up and that her pious, simple mother was part of it.

The new guest, the one who talked the most, spoke with a strange lisp, and Anna didn't like this, either. She stepped smoothly between the men to pick up their plates. She used the excuse of a letter from her brother to go out directly after breakfast. "Mama," she said. "I'll just take John's letter to poor Miss Ward."

Just as her brother enjoyed discouraging her own romantic inclinations, she made it her business to discourage the affections of Miss Ward with regard to him. Calling on Miss Ward with the letter would look like a kindness, but it would make the point that Miss Ward had not gotten a letter herself.

Besides, Booth was in town. If Anna was outside, she might see him again.

The thirteenth had been beautiful, but the weather on the fourteenth was equal parts mud and wind. The wind blew bits of Anna's hair loose and tangled them up with the fringe of her shawl. Around the Treasury Building she stopped to watch a carriage sunk in the mud all the way up to the axle. The horses, a matched pair of blacks, were rescued first. Then planks were laid across the top of the mud for the occupants. They debarked, a man and a woman, the woman unfashionably thin and laughing giddily as with every unsteady step her hoop swung and unbalanced her, first this way and then that. She clutched the man's arm and screamed when a pig burrowed past her, then laughed again at even higher pitch. The man stumbled into the mire when she grabbed him, and this made her laugh, too. The man's clothing was very fine, although now quite speckled with mud. A crowd gathered to watch the woman—the attention made her helpless with laughter.

The war had ended, Anna thought, and everyone had gone simultaneously mad. She was not the only one to think so. It was the subject of newspaper editorials, of barroom speeches. "The city is disorderly with men who are celebrating too hilariously," the president's day guard, William Crook, had written just yesterday. The sun came out, but only in a perfunctory, pale fashion.

Her visit to Miss Ward was spoiled by the fact that John had sent a letter there as well. Miss Ward obviously enjoyed telling Anna so. She was very nearsighted, and she held the letter right up to her eyes to read it. John had recently fled to Canada. With the war over, there was every reason to expect he would come home, even if neither letter said so.

There was more news, and Miss Ward preened while she delivered it. "Lucy Hale is being taken to Spain. Much against her will," Miss Ward said. Lucy was the daughter of ex-senator John P. Hale. Her father hoped that a change of scenery would help pretty Miss Lucy conquer her infatuation for John Wilkes Booth. Miss Ward, whom no one, including Anna's brother, thought was pretty, was laughing at her. "Mr. Hale does not want an actor in the family," Miss Ward said, and Anna regretted the generous impulse that had sent her all the way across town on such a gloomy day.

"Wilkes Booth is back in Washington," Miss Ward finished, and Anna was at least able to say that she knew this; he had called on them only yesterday. She left the Wards with the barest of good-byes.

Karen Joy Fowler

Louis Wiechmann passed her on the street, stopping for a cour-
teous greeting, although they had just seen each other at breakfast. It
was now about ten a.m. Wiechmann was on his way to church. Among
the many secrets he knew was Anna's. "I saw John Wilkes Booth in the
barbershop this morning," he told her. "With a crowd watching his
every move."

Anna raised her head. "Mr. Booth is a famous thespian. Naturally people admire him."

She flattered herself that she knew JW a little better than these
idolaters did. The last time her brother had brought Booth home, he'd
followed Anna out to the kitchen. She'd had her back to the door,
washing the plates. Suddenly she could feel that he was there. How
could she have known that? The back of her neck grew hot, and when
she turned, sure enough, there he was, leaning against the doorjamb,
studying his nails.

"Do you believe our fates are already written?" Booth asked her.
He stepped into the kitchen. "I had my palm read once by a gypsy.
She said I would come to a bad end. She said it was the worst palm
she had ever seen." He held his hand out for her to take. "She said she
wished she hadn't even seen it," he whispered, and then he drew back
quickly as her mother entered, before she could bend over the hand
herself, reassure him with a different reading, before she could even
touch him.

"JW isn't satisfied with acting," her brother had told her once.
"He yearns for greatness on the stage of history." And if her mother
hadn't interrupted, if Anna had had two seconds to herself with him,
this is the reading she would have done. She would have promised him
greatness.

"Mr. Booth was on his way to Ford's Theatre to pick up his mail,"
Wiechmann said with a wink. It was an ambiguous wink. It might
have meant only that Wiechmann remembered what a first love was

like. It might have suggested he knew the use she would make of such information.

Two regiments were returning to Washington from Virginia. They were out of step and out of breath, covered with dust. Anna drew a handkerchief from her sleeve and waved it at them. Other women were doing the same. A crowd gathered. A vendor came through the crowd, selling oysters. A man in a tight-fitting coat stopped him. He had a disreputable look—a bad haircut with long sideburns. He pulled a handful of coins from one pocket and stared at them stupidly. He was drunk. The vendor had to reach into his hand and pick out what he was owed.

"Filthy place!" the man next to the drunk man said. "I really can't bear the smell. I can't eat. Don't expect me to sleep in that flea-infested hotel another night." He left abruptly, colliding with Anna's arm, forcing her to take a step or two. "Excuse me," he said without stopping, and there was nothing penitent or apologetic in his tone. He didn't even seem to see her.

Since he had forced her to start, Anna continued to walk. She didn't even know she was going to Ford's Theatre until she turned onto Eleventh Street. It was a bad idea, but she couldn't seem to help herself. She began to walk faster.

"No tickets, miss," James R. Ford told her, before she could open her mouth. She was not the only one there. A small crowd of people stood at the theater door. "Absolutely sold out. It's because the president and General Grant will be attending."

James Ford held an American flag in his arms. He raised it. "I'm just decorating the president's box." It was the last night of a lackluster run. He would never have guessed they would sell every seat. He thought Anna's face showed disappointment. He was happy, himself, and it made him kind. "They're rehearsing inside," he told her. "For General Grant! You just go on in for a peek."

He opened the doors, and she entered. Three women and a man came with her. Anna had never seen any of the others before, but supposed they were friends of Mr. Ford's. They forced themselves through the doors beside her and then sat next to her in the straight-backed cane chairs just back from the stage.

Laura Keene herself stood in the wings awaiting her entrance. The curtain was pulled back, so that Anna could see her. Her cheeks were round with rouge.

The stage was not deep. Mrs. Mountchessington stood on it with her daughter, Augusta, and Asa Trenchard.

"All I crave is affection," Augusta was saying. She shimmered with insincerity.

Anna repeated the lines to herself. She imagined herself as an actress, married to JW, courted by him daily before an audience of a thousand, in a hundred different towns. They would play the love scenes over and over again, each one as true as the last. She would hardly know where her real and imaginary lives diverged. She didn't suppose there was much money to be made, but even to pretend to be rich seemed like happiness to her.

Augusta was willing to be poor, if she was loved. "Now I've no fortune," Asa said to her in response, "but I'm biling over with affections, which I'm ready to pour out all over you, like apple sass, over roast pork."

The women exited. He was alone on the stage. Anna could see Laura Keene mouthing his line, just as he spoke it. The woman seated next to her surprised her by whispering it aloud as well.

"Well, I guess I know enough to turn you inside out, old gal, you sockdologizing old man-trap," the three of them said. Anna turned to her seatmate, who stared back. Her accent, Anna thought, had been English. "Don't you love theater?" she asked Anna in a whisper. Then her face changed. She was looking at something above Anna's head.

Anna looked, too. Now she understood the woman's expression. John Wilkes Booth was standing in the presidential box, staring down on the actor. Anna rose. Her seatmate caught her arm. She was considerably older than Anna, but not enough so that Anna could entirely dismiss her possible impact on Booth.

"Do you know him?" the woman asked.

"He's a friend of my brother's." Anna had no intention of introducing them. She tried to edge away, but the woman still held her.

"My name is Cassie Streichman."

"Anna Surratt."

There was a quick, sideways movement in the woman's eyes. "Are you related to Mary Surratt?"

"She's my mother." Anna began to feel just a bit of concern. So many people interested in her dull, sad mother. Anna tried to shake loose, and found, to her surprise, that she couldn't. The woman would not let go.

"I've heard of the boarding house," Mrs. Streichman said. It was a courtesy to think of her as a married woman. It was more of a courtesy than she deserved.

Anna looked up at the box again. Booth was already gone. "Let me go," she told Mrs. Streichman, so loudly that Laura Keene herself heard. So forcefully that Mrs. Streichman finally did so.

Anna left the theater. The streets were crowded, and she could not see Booth anywhere. Instead, as she stood on the bricks, looking left and then right, Mrs. Streichman caught up with her. "Are you going home? Might we walk along?"

"No. I have errands," Anna said. She walked quickly away. She was cross now, because she had hoped to stay and look for Booth, who must still be close by, but Mrs. Streichman had made her too uneasy. She looked back once. Mrs. Streichman stood in the little circle of her friends, talking animatedly. She gestured with her hands like a European. Anna saw Booth nowhere.

She went back along the streets to St. Patrick's Church, in search of her mother. It was noon and the air was warm in spite of the colorless sun. Inside the church, her mother knelt in the pew and prayed noisily. Anna slipped in beside her.

"This is the moment," her mother whispered. She reached out and took Anna's hand, gripped it tightly enough to hurt. Her mother's eyes brightened with tears. "This is the moment they nailed him to the cross," she said. There was purple cloth over the crucifix. The pallid sunlight flowed into the church through colored glass.

Across town a group of men had gathered in the Kirkwood bar and were entertaining themselves by buying drinks for George Atzerodt. Atzerodt was one of Booth's co-conspirators. His assignment for the day, given to him by Booth, was to kidnap the vice president. He was already so drunk he couldn't stand. "Would you say that the vice president is a brave man?" he asked, and they laughed at him. He didn't mind being laughed at. It struck him a bit funny himself. "He wouldn't carry a firearm, would he? I mean, why would he?" Atzerodt said. "Are there ever soldiers with him? That nigger who watches him eat. Is he there all the time?"

"Have another drink," they told him, laughing. "On us," and you couldn't get insulted at that.

Anna and her mother returned to the boarding house. Mary Surratt had rented a carriage and was going into the country. "Mr. Wiechmann will drive me," she told her daughter. A Mr. Nothey owed her money they desperately needed; Mary Surratt was going to collect it.

But just as she was leaving, Booth appeared. He took her mother's arm, drew her to the parlor. Anna felt her heart stop and then start again, faster. "Mary, I must talk to you," he said to her mother, whispering, intimate. "Mary." He didn't look at Anna at all and didn't speak again until she left the room. She would have stayed outside the door to hear whatever she could, but Louis Wiechmann had had the same idea. They exchanged one cross look, and then each left the hallway. Anna went up the stairs to her bedroom.

She knew the moment Booth went. She liked to feel that this was because they had a connection, something unexplainable, something preordained, but in fact she could hear the door. He went without asking to see her. She moved to the small window to watch him leave. He did not stop to glance up. He mounted a black horse, tipped his hat to her mother.

Her mother boarded a hired carriage, leaning on Mr. Wiechmann's hand. She held a parcel under her arm. Anna had never seen it before. It was flat and round and wrapped in newspaper. Anna thought it was a gift from Booth. It made her envious.

Later, at her mother's trial, Anna would hear that the package had contained a set of field glasses. A man named Lloyd would testify that Mary Surratt had delivered them to him and had also given him instructions from Booth regarding guns. It was the single most damaging evidence against her. At her brother's trial, Lloyd would recant everything but the field glasses. He was, he now said, too drunk at the time to remember what Mrs. Surratt had told him. He had never remembered. The prosecution had compelled his earlier testimony through threats. This revision would come two years after Mary Surratt had been hanged.

Anna stood at the window a long time, pretending that Booth might return with just such a present for her.

John Wilkes Booth passed George Atzerodt on the street at five p.m. Booth was on horseback. He told Atzerodt he had changed his mind about the kidnapping. He now wanted the vice president killed. At 10:15 or thereabouts. "I've learned that Johnson is a very brave man," Atzerodt told him.

"And you are not," Booth agreed. "But you're in too deep to back out now." He rode away. Booth was carrying in his pocket a letter to the editor of the *National Intelligencer*. In it, he recounted the reasons for Lincoln's death. He had signed his own name, but also that of George Atzerodt.

The men who worked with Atzerodt once said he was a man you could insult and he would take no offense. It was the kindest thing they could think of to say. Three men from the Kirkwood bar appeared and took Atzerodt by the arms. "Let's find another bar," they suggested. "We have hours and hours yet before the night is over. Eat, drink. Be merry."

At six p.m. John Wilkes Booth gave the letter to John Matthews, an actor, asking him to deliver it the next day. "I'll be out of town or I would deliver it myself," he explained. A group of Confederate officers marched down Pennsylvania Avenue where John Wilkes Booth could see them. They were unaccompanied; they were turning themselves in. It was the submissiveness of it that struck Booth hardest. "A man can meet his fate or make it," he told Matthews. "A man can rise to the occasion or fall beneath it."

At sunset, a man called Peanut John lit the big glass globe at the entrance to Ford's Theatre. Inside, the presidential box had been decorated with borrowed flags and bunting. The door into the box had been forced some weeks ago in an unrelated incident and could no longer be locked.

It was early evening when Mary Surratt returned home. Her financial affairs were still unsettled; Mr. Nothey had not even shown up at their meeting. She kissed her daughter. "If Mr. Nothey will not pay us what he owes," she said, "I can't think what we will do next. I can't see a way ahead for us. Your brother must come home." She went into the kitchen to oversee the preparations for dinner.

Anna went in to help. Since the afternoon, since the moment

Booth had not spoken to her, she had been overcome with unhappiness. It had not lessened a bit in the last hours; she now doubted it ever would. She cut the roast into slices. It bled beneath her knife, and she thought of Henrietta Irving's white skin and the red heart beating underneath. She could understand Henrietta Irving perfectly. All I crave is affection, she said to herself, and the honest truth of the sentiment softened her into tears. Perhaps she could survive the rest of her life, if she played it this way, scene by scene. She held the knife up, watching the blood slide down the blade, and this was dramatic and fit her Shakespearian mood.

She felt a chill, and when she turned around one of the new boarders was leaning against the doorjamb, watching her mother. "We're not ready yet," she told him crossly. He'd given her a start. He vanished back into the parlor.

Once again, the new guests hardly ate. Louis Wiechmann finished his food with many elegant compliments. His testimony in court would damage Mary Surratt almost as much as Lloyd's. He would say that she seemed uneasy that night, unsettled, although none of the other boarders saw this. After dinner Mary Surratt went through the house, turning off the kerosene lights one by one.

Anna took a glass of wine and went to sleep immediately. She dreamed deeply, but her heartbreak woke her again only an hour or so later. It stabbed at her lightly from the inside when she breathed. She could see John Wilkes Booth as clearly as if he were in the room with her. "I am the most famous man in America," he said. He held out his hand, beckoned to her.

Downstairs she heard the front door open and close. She rose and looked out the window, just as she had done that afternoon. Many people, far too many people, were on the street. They were all walking in the same direction. One of them was George Atzerodt. Hours before he had abandoned his knife, but he too would die, along

Karen Joy Fowler

with Mary Surratt. He had gone too far to back out. He walked with his hands over the shoulders of two dark-haired men. One of them looked up. He was of a race Anna had never seen before. The new boarders joined the crowd. Anna could see them when they passed out from under the porch overhang.

Something big was happening. Something big enough to overwhelm her own hurt feelings. Anna dressed slowly and then quickly and more quickly. I live, she thought, in the most wondrous of times. Here was the proof. She was still unhappy, but she was also excited. She moved quietly past her mother's door.

The flow of people took her down several blocks. She was taking her last walk again, only backward, like a ribbon uncoiling. She went past St. Patrick's Church, down Eleventh Street. The crowd ended at Ford's Theatre and thickened there. Anna was jostled. To her left, she recognized the woman from the carriage, the laughing woman, though she wasn't laughing now. Someone stepped on Anna's hoop skirt, and she heard it snap. Someone struck her in the back of the head with an elbow. "Be quiet!" someone admonished someone else. "We'll miss it." Someone took hold of her arm. It was so crowded, she couldn't even turn to see, but she heard the voice of Cassie Streichman.

"I had tickets and everything," Mrs. Streichman said angrily. "Do you believe that? I can't even get to the door. It's almost ten o'clock and I had tickets."

"Can my group please stay together?" a woman toward the front asked. "Let's not lose anyone," and then she spoke again in a language Anna did not know.

"It didn't seem a good show," Anna said to Mrs. Streichman. "A comedy and not very funny."

Mrs. Streichman twisted into the space next to her. "That was just a rehearsal. The reviews are incredible. And you wouldn't believe the waiting list. Years. Centuries! I'll never have tickets again." She took a deep, calming breath. "At least you're here, dear. That's something I couldn't have expected. That makes it very real. And," she pressed Anna's arm, "if it helps in any way, you must tell yourself later there's nothing you could have done to make it come out differently. Everything that will happen has already happened. It won't be changed."

"Will I get what I want?" Anna asked her. She could not keep the brightness of hope from her voice. Clearly, she was part of something enormous. Something memorable. How many people could say that?

"I don't know what you want," Mrs. Streichman answered. She had an uneasy look. "I didn't get what I wanted," she added. "Even though I had tickets. Good God! People getting what they want. That's not the history of the world, is it?"

"Will everyone please be quiet!" someone behind Anna said. "Those of us in the back can't hear a thing."

Mrs. Streichman began to cry, which surprised Anna very much. "I'm such a sap," Mrs. Streichman said apologetically. "Things really get to me." She put her arm around Anna.

"All I want," Anna began, but a man to her right hushed her angrily.

"Shut up!" he said. "As if we came all this way to listen to you."

What I Didn't See

I saw Archibald Murray's obituary in the *Tribune* a couple of days ago. It was a long notice, because of all those furbelows he had after his name, and dredged up that old business of ours, which can't have pleased his children. I, myself, have never spoken up before, as I've always felt that nothing I saw sheds any light, but now I'm the last of us. Even Wilmet is gone, though I always picture him such a boy. And there is something to be said for having the last word, which I am surely having.

I still go to the jungle sometimes when I sleep. The sound of the clock turns to a million insects all chewing at once, water dripping onto leaves, the hum inside your head when you run a fever. Sooner or later Eddie comes, in his silly hat and boots up to his knees. He puts his arms around me in the way he did when he meant business, and I wake up too hot, too old, and all alone.

You're never alone in the jungle. You can't see through the twist of roots and leaves and vines, the streakish, tricky light, but you've always got a sense of being seen. You make too much noise when you walk.

At the same time, you understand that you don't matter. You're small and stuck on the ground. The ghosts of paths weren't made for you. If you get bitten by a snake, it's your own damn fault, not the snake's, and if someone doesn't drag you out you'll turn to mulch just like anything else would and show up next as mold or moss, ferns, leeches, ants, millipedes, butterflies, beetles. The jungle is a jammed-alive place, which means that something is always dying there.

Eddie had this idea once that defects of character could be treated with doses of landscape: the ocean for the histrionic, mountains for the domineering, and so forth. I forget the desert, but the jungle was the place to send the self-centered.

We seven went into the jungle with guns in our hands and love in our hearts. I say so now when there is no one left to contradict me.

Archer organized us. He was working at the time for the Louisville Museum of Natural History, and he had a stipend from Collections for skins and bones. The rest of us were amateur enthusiasts and paid our own way just for the adventure. Archer asked Eddie (arachnids) to go along, and Russell MacNamara (chimps), and Trenton Cox (butterflies), who couldn't or wouldn't, and Wilmet Siebert (big game), and Merion Cowper (tropical medicine), and also Merion's wife, only he turned out to be between wives by the time we left, so he was the one who brought Beverly Kriss.

I came with Eddie to help with his nets, pooters, and kill jars. I was never the sort to scream over bugs, but if I had been, twenty-eight years of marriage to Eddie would have cured me. The more legs a creature had, the better Eddie thought of it. Up to point. Up to eight.

In fact Archer was anxious there be some women and had specially invited me, though Eddie didn't tell me so. This was smart; I would have suspected I was along to do the dishes (though of course there were the natives for this) and for nursing the sick, which we did end up at a bit, Beverly and I, when the matter was too small or too nasty for Merion. I might not have come at all if I'd known I was wanted. As it was, I learned to bake a passable bread on campfire coals with a native beer for yeast, but it was my own choice to do so and I ate as much of the bread myself as I wished.

I pass over the various boats on which we sailed, though these trips were not without incident. Wilmet turned out to have a nervous stomach; it started to trouble him on the ocean and then stuck around when we hit dry land again. Russell was a drinker, and not the good sort, unlucky and suspicious, a man who thought he loved a game of cards, but should have never been allowed to play. Beverly was a modern girl in 1928 and could chew gum, smoke, and wipe the lipstick off her mouth and onto yours all at the same time. She and Merion were frisky for Archer's taste, and he tried to shift this off onto me, saying I was being made uncomfortable, when I didn't care one way or the other. I worried that it would be a pattern, and every time one of the men was tired on the trail they'd say we had to stop on my account. I told Eddie right away I wouldn't like it if this was to happen. So by the time we were geared up and walking in, we already thought we knew each other pretty well, and we didn't entirely like what we knew. Still, I guessed we'd get along fine when there was more to occupy us. Even during those long days it took to reach the mountains—the endless trains, motor cars, donkeys, mules, and finally our very own feet—things went smoothly enough.

By the time we reached the Lulenga Mission, we'd seen a fair bit of Africa—low and high, hot and cold, black and white. I've learned some things in the years since, so there's a strong temptation now to pretend that I felt the things I should have felt, knew the things I might have known. The truth is otherwise. My attitudes toward the natives, in particular, were not what they might have been. The men who helped us interested me little and impressed me not at all. Many of them had their teeth filed and were only ten years or so from cannibalism, or so we were informed. No one, ourselves included, was clean, but Beverly and I would have tried, only we couldn't bathe without the nuisance of being spied on. Whether this was to see if we looked good or only good to eat, I did not wish to know.

The fathers at the mission told us that slaves used to be led through the villages in ropes so that people could draw on their bodies the cuts of meat they were buying before the slaves were butchered, and with that my mind was set. I never did acknowledge any beauty or kindness in the people we met, though Eddie saw much of both.

We spent three nights in Lulenga, which gave us each a bed, good food, and a chance to wash our hair and clothes in some privacy. Beverly and I shared a room, there not being sufficient number for her to have her own. She was quarreling with Merion at the time, though I forget about what. They were a tempest, those two, always shouting, sulking, and then turning on the heat again. A tiresome sport for spectators, but surely invigorating for the players. So Eddie was bunked up with Russell, which put me out, because I liked to wake up with him.

We were joined at dinner the first night by a Belgian administrator who treated us to real wine and whose name I no longer remember, though I can picture him yet—a bald, hefty man in his sixties with a white beard. I recall how he joked that his hair had migrated from his head to his chin and then settled in where the food was plentiful.

Eddie was in high spirits and talking more than usual. The spiders in Africa are exhilaratingly aggressive. Many of them have fangs and nocturnal habits. We'd already shipped home dozens of button spiders with red hourglasses on their backs, and some beautiful golden violin spiders with long delicate legs and dark chevrons underneath. But that evening Eddie was most excited about a small jumping spider, which seemed not to spin her own web, but to lurk instead in the web of another. She had no beautiful markings; when he'd first seen one, he'd thought she was a bit of dirt blown into the silken strands. Then she grew legs and, as we watched, stalked and killed the web's owner and all with a startling cunning.

"Working together, a thousand spiders can tie up a lion," the Belgian told us. Apparently it was a local saying. "But then they don't work together, do they? The blacks haven't noticed. Science is observation, and Africa produces no scientists."

In those days all gorilla hunts began at Lulenga, so it took no great discernment to guess that the rest of our party was not after spiders. The Belgian told us that only six weeks past, a troupe of gorilla males had attacked a tribal village. The food stores had been broken into and a woman carried off. Her bracelets were found the next day, but she'd not yet returned, and the Belgian feared she never would. It was such a sustained siege that the whole village had to be abandoned.

"The seizure of the woman I dismiss as superstition and exaggeration," Archer said. He had a formal way of speaking; you'd never guess he was from Kentucky. Not so grand to look at—inch-thick glasses that made his eyes pop, unkempt hair, filthy shirt cuffs. He poured more of the Belgian's wine around, and I recall his being especially generous to his own glass. Isn't it funny, the things you remember? "But the rest of your story interests me. If any gorilla was taken I'd pay for the skin, assuming it wasn't spoiled in the peeling."

The Belgian said he would inquire. And then he persisted with his main point, very serious and deliberate. "As to the woman, I've heard these tales too often to discard them so quickly as you. I've heard of native women subjected to degradations far worse than death. May I ask you as a favor, then, in deference to my greater experience and longer time here, to leave your women at the mission when you go gorilla hunting?"

It was courteously done and obviously cost Archer to refuse. Yet he did, saying to my astonishment that it would defeat his whole purpose to leave me and Beverly behind. He then gave the Belgian his own thinking, which we seven had already heard over several repetitions—that gorillas were harmless and gentle, if oversized and overmuscled. Sweet-natured vegetarians. He based this entirely on the wear on their teeth; he'd read a paper on it from some university in London.

Archer then characterized the famous Du Chaillu description—glaring eyes, yellow incisors, hellish dream creatures—as a slick and dangerous form of self-aggrandizement. It was an account tailored to bring big game hunters on the run and so had to be quickly countered for the gorillas' own protection. Archer was out to prove Du Chaillu wrong, and he needed me and Beverly to help. "If one of the girls should bring down a large male," he said, "it will seem as exciting as shooting a cow. No man will cross a continent merely to do something a pair of girls has already done."

He never did ask us, because that wasn't his way. He just raised it as our Christian duty and then left us to worry it over in our minds.

Of course we were all carrying rifles. Eddie and I had practiced on bottles and such in preparation for the trip. On the way over I'd gotten pretty good at clay pigeons off the deck of our ship. But I wasn't eager to kill a gentle vegetarian—a nightmare from hell would have suited me a good deal better (if scared me a great deal more). Beverly, too, I'm guessing.

Not that she said anything about it that night. Wilmet, our youngest at twenty-five years and also shortest by a whole head—blond hair, pink cheeks, and little rat's eyes—had been lugging a tin of British biscuits about the whole trip and finishing every dinner by eating one while we watched. He was always explaining why they couldn't be shared when no one was asking. They kept his stomach settled; he couldn't afford to run out and so on; his very life might depend on them if he were sick and nothing else would stay down and so forth. We wouldn't have noticed if he hadn't persisted in bringing it up.

But suddenly he and Beverly had their heads close together, whispering, and he was giving her one of his precious biscuits. She took it without so much as a glance at Merion, even when he leaned in to say he'd like one, too. Wilmet answered that there were too few to share with everyone, so Merion upset a water glass into the tin and spoiled all the biscuits that remained. Wilmet left the table and didn't return, and the subject of the all-girl gorilla hunt passed by in the unpleasantness.

That night I woke under the gauze of the mosquito net in such a heat I thought I had malaria. Merion had given us all quinine, and I meant to take it regularly, but I didn't always remember. There are worse fevers in the jungle, especially if you've been collecting spiders, so it was cheerful of me to fix on malaria. My skin was burning from the inside out, especially my hands and feet, and I was sweating like butter on a hot day. I thought to wake Beverly, but by the time I stood up the fit had already passed, and anyway her bed was empty.

In the morning she was back. I planned to talk to her then, get her thoughts on gorilla hunting, but I woke early and she slept late.

I breakfasted alone and went for a stroll around the Mission grounds. It was cool, with little noise beyond the wind and birds. To the west, a dark trio of mountains, two of which smoked. Furrowed fields below me, banana plantations, and trellises of roses curving into archways that led to the church. How often we grow a garden around our houses of worship. We march ourselves through Eden to get to God.

Merion joined me in the graveyard, where I'd just counted three deaths by lion, British names all. I was thinking how outlandish it was, how sadly unlikely that all the prams and nannies and public schools should come to this, and even the bodies pinned under stones so hyenas wouldn't come for them. I was hoping for a more modern sort of death myself, a death at home, a death from American causes, when Merion cleared his throat behind me.

He didn't look like my idea of a doctor, but I believe he was a good one. Well-paid, that's for sure and certain. As to appearances, he reminded me of the villain in some Lillian Gish film, meaty and needing a shave, but handsome enough when cleaned up. He swung his arms when he walked, so he took up more space than he needed. There was something to this confidence I admired, though it irritated me on principle. I often liked him least of all and I'm betting he was sharp enough to know it. "I trust you slept well," he said. He looked at me slantwise, looked away again. *I trust you slept well. I trust you were in no way disturbed by Beverly sneaking out to meet me in the middle of the night.*

Or maybe—*I trust Beverly didn't sneak out last night.*

Or maybe just *I trust you slept well.* It wasn't a question, which saved me the nuisance of figuring the answer.

"So," he said next, "what do you think of this gorilla scheme of Archer's?" And then gave me no time to respond. "The fathers tell me a party from Manchester went up just last month and brought back seventeen. Four of them youngsters—lovely little family group for the British museum. I only hope they left us a few." And then, lowering his voice, "I'm glad for the chance to discuss things with you privately."

There turned out to be a detail to the Belgian's story judged too delicate for the dinnertable, but Merion, being a doctor and maybe more of a man's man than Archer, a man who could be appealed to on behalf of women, had heard it. The woman carried away from the village had been menstruating. This at least the Belgian hoped, that we'd not to go up the mountain with our female affliction in full flower.

And because he was a doctor I told Merion straight out that I'd been light and occasional; I credited this to the upset of travel. I thought to set his mind at ease, but I should have guessed I wasn't his first concern.

"Beverly's too headstrong to listen to me," he said. "Too young and reckless. She'll take her cue from you. A solid, sensible, mature woman like you could rein her in a bit. For her own good."

A woman unlikely to inflame the passions of jungle apes was what I heard. Even in my prime I'd never been the sort of woman poems are written about, but this seemed to place me low indeed. An hour later I saw the humor in it, and Eddie surely laughed at me quickly enough when I confessed it, but at the time I was sincerely insulted. How sensible, how mature was that?

I was further provoked by the way he expected me to give in. Archer was certain I'd agree to save the gorillas, and Merion was certain I'd agree to save Beverly. I had a moment's outrage over these men who planned to run me by appealing to what they imagined was my weakness.

Merion more than Archer. How smug he was, and how I detested his calm acceptance of every advantage that came to him, as if it were no more than his due. No white woman in all the world had seen the wild gorillas yet—we were to be the first—but I was to step aside from it just because he asked me.

"I haven't walked all this way to miss out on the gorillas," I told him, as politely as I could. "The only question is whether I'm looking or shooting at them." And then I left him, because my own feelings were no credit to me and I didn't mean to have them anymore. I went to look for Eddie and spend the rest of the day emptying kill jars, pinning and labeling the occupants.

The next morning Beverly announced, in deference to Merion's wishes, that she'd be staying behind at the mission when we went on. Quick as could be, Wilmet said his stomach was in such an uproar that he would stay behind as well. This took us all by surprise as he was the only real hunter among us. And it put Merion in an awful bind—we'd more likely need a doctor on the mountain than at the mission, but I guessed he'd sooner see Beverly taken by gorillas than by Wilmet. He fussed and sweated over a bunch of details that didn't matter to anyone and all the while the day passed in secret conferences—Merion with Archer, Archer with Beverly, Russell with Wilmet, Eddie with Beverly. By dinnertime Beverly said she'd changed her mind, and Wilmet had undergone a wonderful recovery. When we left next morning we were at full complement, but pretty tightly strung.

It took almost two hundred porters to get our little band of seven up Mount Mikeno. It was a hard track with no path, hoisting ourselves over roots, cutting and crawling our way through tightly woven bamboo. There were long slides of mud on which it was impossible to get a grip. And always sharp uphill. My heart and my lungs worked as hard or harder than my legs, and though it wasn't hot I had to wipe my face and neck continually. As the altitude rose I gasped for breath like a fish in a net.

We women were placed in the middle of the pack with gun-bearers both ahead and behind. I slid back many times and had to be caught and set upright again. Eddie was in a torment over the webs we walked through with no pause as to architect and Russell over the bearers who, he guaranteed, would bolt with our guns at the first sign of danger. But we wouldn't make camp if we stopped for spiders and couldn't stay the course without our hands free. Soon Beverly sang out for a gorilla to come and carry her the rest of the way.

Then we were all too winded and climbed for hours without speaking, breaking whenever we came suddenly into the sun, sustaining ourselves with chocolate and crackers.

Still our mood was excellent. We saw elephant tracks, large, sunken bowls in the mud, half-filled with water. We saw glades of wild carrots and an extravagance of pink and purple orchids. Grasses in greens so delicate they seemed to be melting. I revised my notions of Eden, leaving the roses behind and choosing instead these remote forests where the gorillas lived—foggy rains, the crooked hagenia trees strung with vines, golden mosses, silver lichen; the rattle and buzz of flies and beetles; the smell of catnip as we stepped into it.

At last we stopped. Our porters set up, which gave us a chance to rest. My feet were swollen and my knees stiffening, but I had a great appetite for dinner and a great weariness for bed; I was asleep before sundown. And then I was awake again. The temperature, which had been pleasant all day, plunged. Eddie and I wrapped ourselves in coats and sweaters and each other. He worried about our porters, who didn't have the blankets we had, although they were free to keep a fire up as high as they liked. At daybreak, they came complaining to Archer. He raised their pay a dime apiece since they had surely suffered during the night, but almost fifty of them left us anyway.

We spent that morning sitting around the camp, nursing our blisters and scrapes, some of us looking for spiders, some of us practicing our marksmanship. There was a stream about five minutes walk away with a pool where Beverly and I dropped our feet. No mosquitoes, no sweat bees, no flies, and that alone made it paradise. But no sooner did I have this thought than a wave of malarial heat came on me, drenching the back of my shirt.

When I came to myself again, Beverly was in the middle of something, and I hadn't heard the beginning. She might have told me Merion's former wife had been unfaithful to him. Later this seemed like something I'd once been told, but maybe only because it made sense. "Now he seems to think the apes will leave me alone if only I don't go tempting them," she said. "Lord!"

"He says they're drawn to menstrual blood."

"Then I've got no problem. Anyway Russell says that Burunga says we'll never see them, dressed as we're dressed. Our clothes make too much noise when we walk. He told Russell we must hunt them naked. I haven't passed that on to Merion yet. I'm saving it for a special occasion."

I had no idea who Burunga was. Not the cook and not our chief guide, which were the only names I'd bothered with. I was, at least (and I do see now, how very least it is) embarrassed to learn that Beverly had done otherwise. "Are you planning to shoot an ape?" I asked. It came over me all of sudden that I wanted a particular answer, but I couldn't unearth what answer that was.

"I'm not really a killer," she said. "More a sweet-natured vegetarian. Of the meat-eating variety. But Archer says he'll put my picture up in the museum. You know the sort of thing—rifle on shoulder, foot on body, eyes to the horizon. Wouldn't that be something to take the kiddies to?"

Eddie and I had no kiddies; Beverly might have realized it was a sore spot. And Archer had made no such representations to me. She sat in a spill of sunlight. Her hair was short and heavy and fell in a neat cap over her ears. Brown until the sun made it golden. She wasn't a pretty woman so much as she just drew your eye and kept it. "Merion keeps on about how he paid my way here. Like he hasn't gotten his money's worth." She kicked her feet, and water beaded up on her bare legs. "You're so lucky. Eddie's the best."

Which he was, and any woman could see it. I never met a better man than my Eddie, and in our whole forty-three years together there were only three times I wished I hadn't married him. I say this now, because we're coming up on one of those times. I wouldn't want someone thinking less of Eddie because of anything I said.

"You're still in love with him, aren't you?" Beverly asked. "After so many years of marriage."

I admitted as much.

Beverly shook her golden head. "Then you'd best keep with him," she told me.

Or did she? What did she say to me? I've been over the conversation so many times I no longer remember it at all.

In contrast, this next bit is perfectly clear. Beverly said she was tired and went to her tent to lie down. I found the men playing bridge, taking turns at watching. I was bullied into playing, because Russell didn't like his cards and thought to change his luck by putting some empty space between hands. So it was me and Wilmet opposite Eddie and Russell, with Merion and Archer in the vicinity, smoking and looking on. On the other side of the tents the laughter of our porters.

I would have liked to team with Eddie, but Russell said bridge was too dangerous a game when husbands and wives partnered up and there was a ready access to guns. He was joking, of course, but you couldn't have told by his face.

While we played, Russell talked about chimpanzees and how they ran their lives. Back in those days no one had looked at chimps yet, so it was all only guesswork. Topped by guessing that gorillas would be pretty much the same. There was a natural order to things, Russell said, and you could reason it out; it was simple Darwinism.

I didn't think you could reason out spiders; I didn't buy that you could reason out chimps. So I didn't listen. I played my cards and every so often a word would fall in. Male this, male that. Blah, blah, dominance. Survival of the fittest, blah, blah. Natural selection, nature red in tooth and claw. Blah and blah. There was an argument then as to whether by simple Darwinism we could expect a social arrangement of monogamous married couples or whether the males would all have harems. There were points to be made either way, and I didn't care for any of those points.

Wilmet opened with one heart and soon we were up to three. I mentioned how Beverly had said she'd get her picture in the Louisville Museum if she killed an ape. "It's not entirely my decision," Archer said. "But, yes, part of my plan is that there will be pictures. And interviews. Possibly in magazines, certainly in the museum. The whole object is that people be told." And this began a discussion over whether, for the purposes of saving gorilla lives, it would work best if Beverly was to kill one or if it should be me. There was some general concern that the sight of Beverly in a pith helmet might be, somehow, stirring, whereas if I were the one, it wouldn't be cute in the least. If Archer really wished to put people off gorilla-hunting, then, the men agreed, I was his girl. Of course it was not as bald as that, but that was the gist.

Wilmet lost a trick he'd hoped to finesse. We were going down, and I suddenly saw that he'd opened with only four hearts, which, though they were pretty enough, an ace and a king included, was a witless thing to do. I still think so.

"I expected more support," he said to me, "when you took us to two," as if it were my fault.

"Length is strength," I said right back, and then I burst into tears, because he was so short it was an awful thing to say. It took me more by surprise than anyone, and most surprising of all, I didn't seem to care about the crying. I got up from the table and walked off. I could hear Eddie apologizing behind me as if I were the one who'd opened with four hearts. "Change of life," I heard him saying. It was so like Eddie to know what was happening to me even before I did.

It was so unlike him to apologize for me. At that moment I hated him with all the rest. I went to our tent and fetched some water and my rifle. We weren't any of us to go into the jungle alone, so no one imagined this was what I was doing.

The sky had begun to cloud up and soon the weather was colder. There was no clear track to follow, only antelope trails. Of course I got lost. I had thought to take every possible turn to the right and then reverse this coming back, but the plan didn't suit the landscape nor achieve the end desired. I had a whistle, but was angry enough not to use it. I counted on Eddie to find me eventually as he always did.

I believe I walked for more than four hours. Twice it rained, intensifying all the green smells of the jungle. Occasionally the sun was out and the mosses and leaves overlaid with silvered water. I saw a cat print that made me move my rifle off of safe to ready and then often had to set it aside as the track took me over roots and under hollow trees. The path was unstable and sometimes slid out from under me.

Once I put my hand on a spider's web. It was a domed web over an orb, intricate and a beautiful pale yellow in color. I never touched a silk so strong. The spider was big and black with yellow spots at the undersides of her legs, and, judging by the corpses, she carried all her victims to the web's center before wrapping them. I would have brought her back, but I had nothing to keep her in. It seemed a betrayal of Eddie to let her be, but that sort of evened our score.

Next thing I put my hand on was a soft-looking leaf. I pulled it away full of nettles.

Although the way back to camp was clearly downhill, I began to go up. I thought to find a vista, see the mountains, orient myself. I was less angry by now and suffered more from the climbing as a result. The rain began again, and I picked out a sheltered spot to sit and tend my stinging hand. I should have been cold and frightened, but I wasn't either. The pain in my hand was subsiding. The jungle was beautiful and the sound of rain a lullaby. I remember wishing that this was where I belonged, that I lived here. Then the heat came on me so hard I couldn't wish at all.

A noise brought me out of it—a crashing in the bamboo. Turning, I saw the movement of leaves and the backside of something rather like a large black bear. A gorilla has a strange way of walking—on the hind feet and the knuckles, but with arms so long their backs are hardly bent. I had one clear look and then the creature was gone. But I could still hear it, and I was determined to see it again.

I knew I'd never have another chance; even if we did see one later the men would take it over. I was still too hot. My shirt was drenched from sweat and rain; my pants, too, and making a noise whenever I bent my knees. So I removed everything and put back only my socks and boots. I left the rest of my clothes folded on the spot where I'd been sitting, picked up my rifle, and went into the bamboo.

Around a rock, under a log, over a root, behind a tree was the prettiest open meadow you'd ever hope to see. Three gorillas were in it, one male, two female. It might have been a harem. It might have been a family—a father, mother, and daughter. The sun came out. One female combed the other with her hands, the two of them blinking in the sun. The male was seated in a patch of wild carrots, pulling and eating them with no particular ardor. I could see his profile and the gray in his fur. He twitched his fingers a bit, like a man listening to music. There were flowers—pink and white—in concentric circles where some pond had been and now wasn't. One lone tree. I stood and looked for a good long time.

Then I raised the barrel of my gun. The movement brought the eyes of the male to me. He stood. He was bigger than I could ever have imagined. In the leather of his face I saw surprise, curiosity, caution. Something else, too. Something so human it made me feel like an old woman with no clothes on. I might have shot him just for that, but

I knew it wasn't right—to kill him merely because he was more human than I anticipated. He thumped his chest, a rhythmic beat that made the women look to him. He showed me his teeth. Then he turned and took the women away.

I watched it all through the sight of my gun. I might have hit him several times—spared the women, freed the women. But I couldn't see that they wanted freeing, and Eddie had told me never to shoot a gun angry. The gorillas faded from the meadow. I was cold then, and I went for my clothes.

Russell had beaten me to them. He stood with two of our guides, staring down at my neatly folded pants. Nothing for it but to walk up beside him and pick them up, shake them for ants, put them on. He turned his back as I dressed, and he couldn't manage a word. I was even more embarrassed. "Eddie must be frantic," I said to break the awkwardness.

"All of us, completely beside ourselves. Did you find any sign of her?"

Which was how I learned that Beverly had disappeared.

We were closer to camp than I'd feared if farther than I'd hoped. While we walked I did my best to recount my final conversation with Beverly to Russell. I was, apparently, the last to have seen her. The card game had broken up soon after I left and the men gone their separate ways. A couple of hours later, Merion began looking for Beverly, who was no longer in her tent. No one was alarmed, at first, but by now they were.

I was made to repeat everything she'd said again and again and questioned over it, too, though there was nothing useful in it and soon I began to feel I'd made up every word. Archer asked our guides to look over the ground about the pool and around her tent. He had some cowboy scene in his mind, I suppose, the primitive who can read a broken branch, a footprint, a bit of fur, and piece it all together. Our guides looked with great seriousness, but found nothing. We searched and called and sent up signaling shots until night came over us.

"She was taken by the gorillas," Merion told us. "Just as I said she'd be." I tried to read his face in the red of the firelight, but couldn't. Nor catch his tone of voice.

"No prints," our chief guide repeated. "No sign."

That night our cook refused to make us dinner. The natives were talking a great deal amongst themselves, very quiet. To us they said as little as possible. Archer demanded an explanation, but got nothing but dodge and evasion.

"They're scared," Eddie said, but I didn't see this.

A night even more bitter than the last and Beverly not dressed for it. In the morning the porters came to Archer to say they were going back. No measure of arguing or threatening or bribing changed their minds. We could come or stay as we chose; it was clearly of no moment to them. I, of course, was given no choice, but was sent back to the mission with the rest of the gear, excepting what the men kept behind.

At Lulenga one of the porters tried to speak with me. He had no English, and I followed none of it except Beverly's name. I told him to wait while I fetched one of the fathers to translate, but he misunderstood or else he refused. When we returned he was gone and I never did see him again.

The men stayed eight more days on Mount Mikeno and never found so much as a bracelet.

Because I'm a woman I wasn't there for the parts you want most to hear. The waiting and the not-knowing were, in my view of things, as hard or harder than the searching, but you don't make stories out of that. Something happened to Beverly, but I can't tell you what. Something happened on the mountain after I left, something that brought Eddie back to me so altered in spirit I felt I hardly knew him, but I wasn't there to see what it was. Eddie and I departed Africa immediately and not in the company of the other men in our party. We didn't even pack up all our spiders.

For months after, I wished to talk about Beverly, to put together this possibility and that possibility and settle on something I could live with. I felt the need most strongly at night. But Eddie couldn't hear her name. He'd sunk so deep into himself, he rarely looked out. He stopped sleeping and wept from time to time, and these were things he did his best to hide from me. I tried to talk to him about it, I tried to be patient and loving, I tried to be kind. I failed in all these things.

A year, two more passed, and he began to resemble himself again, but never in full. My full, true Eddie never did come back from the jungle.

Then one day, at breakfast, with nothing particular to prompt it, he told me there'd been a massacre. That after I left for Lulenga the men had spent the days hunting and killing gorillas. He didn't describe it to me at all, yet it sprang bright and terrible into my mind, my own little family group lying in their blood in the meadow.

Forty or more, Eddie said. Probably more. Over several days. Babies, too. They couldn't even bring the bodies back; it looked so bad to be collecting when Beverly was gone. They'd slaughtered the gorillas as if they were cows.

Eddie was dressed in his old plaid robe, his gray hair in uncombed bunches, crying into his fried eggs. I wasn't talking, but he put his hands over his ears in case I did. He was shaking all over from weeping, his head trembling on his neck. "It felt like murder," he said. "Just exactly like murder."

I took his hands down from his head and held on hard. "I expect it was mostly Merion."

"No," he said. "It was mostly me."

At first, Eddie told me, Merion was certain the gorillas had taken Beverly. But later, he began to comment on the strange behavior of the porters. How they wouldn't talk to us, but whispered to each other. How they left so quickly. "I was afraid," Eddie told me. "So upset about Beverly and then terribly afraid. Russell and Merion, they were so angry I could smell it. I thought at any moment one of them would say something that couldn't be unsaid, something that would get to the Belgians. And then I wouldn't be able to stop it anymore. So I kept us stuck on the gorillas. I kept us going after them. I kept us angry until we had killed so very many and were all so ashamed, there would be no way to turn and accuse someone new."

I still didn't quite understand. "Do you think one of the porters killed Beverly?" It was a possibility that had occurred to me, too; I admit it.

"No," said Eddie. "That's my point. But you saw how the blacks were treated back at Lulenga. You saw the chains and the beatings. I couldn't let them be suspected." His voice was so clogged I could hardly make out the words. "I need you to tell me I did the right thing."

So I told him. I told him he was the best man I ever knew. "Thank you," he said. And with that he shook off my hands, dried his eyes, and left the table.

That night I tried to talk to him again. I tried to say that there was nothing he could do that I wouldn't forgive. "You've always been too easy on me," he answered. And the next time I brought it up, "If you love me, we'll never talk about this again."

—∞—

Eddie died three years later without another word on the subject passing between us. In the end, to be honest, I suppose I found that silence rather unforgivable. His death even more so. I have never liked being alone.

As every day I more surely am; it's the blessing of a long life. Just me left now, the first white woman to see the wild gorillas and the one who saw nothing else—not the chains, not the beatings, not the massacre. I can't help worrying over it all again, now I know Archer's dead and only me to tell it, though no way of telling puts it to rest.

Since my eyes went, a girl comes to read to me twice a week. For the longest time I wanted nothing to do with gorillas, but now I have her scouting out articles, as we're finally starting to really see how they live. The thinking still seems to be harems, but with the females slipping off from time to time to be with whomever they wish.

And what I notice most in the articles is not the apes. My attention is caught instead by these young women who'd sooner live in the jungle with the chimpanzees or the orangutans or the great mountain gorillas. These women who freely choose it—the Goodalls and the Galdikases and the Fosseys. And I think to myself how there is nothing new under the sun, and maybe all those women carried off by gorillas in those old stories, maybe they all freely chose it.

When I am tired and have thought too much about it all, Beverly's last words come back to me. Mostly I put them straight out of my head, think about anything else. Who remembers what she said? Who knows what she meant?

But there are other times when I let them in. Turn them over. Then they become, not a threat as I originally heard them, but an invitation. On those days I can pretend that she's still there in the jungle, dipping her feet, eating wild carrots, and waiting for me. I can pretend that I'll be joining her whenever I wish and just as soon as I please.

King Rat

One day when I was in the first grade, Scott Arnold told me he was going to wash my face with snow on my way home from school. By playground rules he couldn't hit a girl, but there was nothing to prevent him from chasing me for blocks, knocking me over and sitting on me while stuffing ice down my neck, and this was what he planned to do. I forget why.

I spent the afternoon with the taste of dread in my mouth. Scott Arnold was a lot bigger than I was. So was everybody else. I was the smallest girl in my first grade class and smaller than most of the kindergartners, too. So I decided not to go home at all. Instead I would surprise my father with a visit to his office.

My school was about halfway between my home and the university where my father worked. I left by a back door. There was snow in the gutters and the yards, but the sidewalks were clear, the walking easy. The university was only five blocks away, and a helpful adult took me across the one busy street. I found the psychology building with no trouble; I'd been there many times with my dad.

The ornate entrance door was too heavy for me. I had to sit on the cold steps until someone else opened it and let me slip inside. If I'd been with my father, we would have taken the elevator to his office on the fourth floor. He might have remembered to lift me up so that

Karen Joy Fowler

I could be the one to press the fourth-floor button. If no one lifted me, I couldn't reach it.

I took the stairs instead. I didn't know that it took two flights to go one floor; I counted carefully but exited too early. There was nothing to tip me off to this. The halls of the first and the second and the third floors looked exactly like those of the fourth: green paint on the walls, flyers, a drinking fountain, rows of wooden doors on both sides.

I knocked on what I believed was my father's office, and a man I didn't know opened it. Apparently he thought I'd interrupted him as a prank. "You shouldn't be wandering around here," he said angrily. "I've half a mind to call the police." The man banged the door shut, and the sharp noise combined with my embarrassment made me cry. I was dressed for snow, and so I was also getting uncomfortably hot.

I retreated to the stairwell, where I sat awhile, crying and thinking. In the lobby of the entryway a giant globe was set into the floor. I loved to spin it, close my eyes, put my finger down on Asia or Ecuador or the painted oceans. I thought that perhaps I could go back to the entrance, find the globe again, start all over. I couldn't imagine where I'd made my mistake, but I thought I could manage not to repeat it. I'd been to my father's office so many times.

But I couldn't stop crying, and this humiliated me more than anything. Only babies cried, Scott Arnold said, whenever he'd made me do so. I did my best not to let anyone see me, waited until the silence in the stairwell persuaded me it was empty before I went back down.

Then I couldn't find the globe again. Every door I tried opened on a green hallway and a row of identical wooden doors. It seemed I couldn't even manage to leave the building. I was more and more frightened. Even if I could find my father's office, I would never dare knock for fear the other man would be the one to answer.

I decided to go to the basement, where the animal lab was. My father might be there or one of his students, someone I knew. I took the stairs as far down as they went and opened the door.

The light was different in the basement—no windows—and the smell was different, too. Fur and feces and disinfectant. I'd been there dozens of times. I knew to skirt the monkeys' cages. I knew they would rattle the bars, show me their teeth, howl, and if I came close enough, they would reach through to grab me. Monkeys were strong for all they were so small. They would bite.

Behind the monkeys were the rats. Their cages were stacked one on the next, so many of them they formed aisles like in the grocery store.

There was never more than a single rat in a single cage. They shredded the newspaper lining and made themselves damp, smelly-confetti nests. When I passed they came out of these nests to look at me, their paws wrapped over the bars, their noses ticking busily from side to side. These were hooded rats with black faces and tiny, nibbling teeth. I felt that their eyes were sympathetic. I felt that they were worried to see me there, lost without my father, and this concern was a comfort to me.

At the end of one of the aisles I found a man I didn't know. He was tall and blond, with pale blue eyes. He knelt and shook my hand so my empty mitten, tied to my sleeve, bounced about in the air. "I'm a stranger here," he said. He pronounced the words oddly. "Newly arrived. So I don't know everyone the way I should. My name is Vidkun Thrane." A large hooded rat climbed out of his shirt pocket. It looked at me with the same worried eyes the caged rats had shown. "I'm not entirely without friends," the blond man said. "Here is King Rat, come to make your acquaintance."

Because of his eyes, I told King Rat my father's name. We all took the elevator up to the fourth floor together.

Karen Joy Fowler

My rescuer was a Norwegian psychologist who'd just come to work in the United States with men like my father, studying theories of learning by running rats through mazes. In Oslo, Vidkun had a wife and a son who was just the age of my older brother. My father was very glad to see him. Me, he was less glad to see.

I cared too much about my dignity to mention Scott Arnold. The door I had knocked on earlier was the office of the department chair, a man who, my father said, already had it in for him. I was told never to come as a surprise to see him again. Vidkun was told to come to supper.

Vidkun visited us several times during his residency, and even came to our Christmas dinner since his own family was so far away. He gave me a book, *Castles and Dragons, A Collection of Fairytales from Many Lands*. I don't know how he chose it. Perhaps the clerk recommended it. Perhaps his son had liked it.

However he found it, it turned out to be the perfect book for me. I read it over and over. It satisfied me in a way no other book ever has, grew up with me the way a good book does. These, then, are the two men I credit with making me a writer. First, my father, a stimulus/response psychologist who believed in reinforcement in the lab, but whose parenting ran instead to parables and medicinal doses of Aesop's fables.

Second, a man I hardly knew, a stranger from very far away, who showed me his home on the large, spinning globe and, one Christmas, brought me the book I wanted above all others to read. I have so few other memories of Vidkun. A soft voice and a gentle manner. The worried eyes of King Rat looking out from his pocket. The unfortunate same first name, my father told me later, as the famous Norwegian traitor. That can't have been easy growing up, I remember my father saying.

The stories in *Castles and Dragons* are full of magical incident. Terrible things may happen before the happy ending, but there are limits to how terrible. Good people get their reward; so do bad people. The stories are much softer than Grimm and Andersen. It was many, many years before I was tough enough for the pure thing.

Even now some of the classics remain hard for me. Of these, worst by a good margin is "The Pied Piper of Hamlin." I never liked the first part with the rats. I saw King Rat and all the others dancing to their doom with their busy noses and worried eyes. Next, I hated the lying parents. And most of all, I hated the ending.

My father always tried to comfort me. The children were wonderfully happy at the end, he said. They were guests at an eternal birthday party where the food was spun sugar and the music just as sweet. They never stopped eating long enough to think of how their parents must miss them.

I wasn't persuaded. By my own experience, on Halloween there always came a moment when you'd eaten too much candy. One by one the children would remember their homes. One by one they would leave the table determined to find their way out of the mountain. They would climb the carved stairs up and then down into darkness. They would lose themselves in caves and stony corridors until their only choice, eventually and eternally, was to follow the music back to the piper. It was not a story with an ending at all. In my mind it stretched horribly onward.

Shortly after I met Vidkun, I wrote my own book. This was an illustrated collection of short pieces. The protagonists were all baby animals. In these stories a pig or a puppy or a lamb wandered inadvertently away from the family. After a frightening search, the stray was found again; a joyful reunion took place. The stories got progressively shorter as the book went on. My parents thought I was running out of energy for it. In fact, I was less and less able to bear the middle part of the story. In each successive version, I made the period of separation shorter.

I can guess now, as I couldn't then, what sorts of things may have happened to the monkeys in the psych lab. I suppose that the rats' lives were not entirely taken up with cheese, tucked into mazes like Easter eggs. As I grew up, there were more and more questions I thought of but didn't ask. Real life is only for the very toughest.

My brother went away to college, and I cried for three days. In his junior year, he went farther, to the south of England and an exchange program at Sussex University. During spring break, he went to Norway on a skiing vacation. He found himself alone at Easter, and he called the only person in all of Norway that he knew.

Vidkun insisted my brother come stay with him and his wife, immediately drove to the hostel to fetch him. He had wonderful memories of our family, he said. He'd spoken of us often. He asked after me. He was cordial and gracious, my brother told me, genuinely welcoming, and yet, clearly something was terribly wrong. My brother had never imagined a house so empty. Easter dinner was long and lavish and cheerless. Sometime during it, Vidkun stopped talking. His wife went early to bed and left the two men sitting at the table.

"My son," Vidkun said suddenly. "My son also took a trip abroad. Like you. He went to America, which I always told him was so wonderful. He went two years ago." Vidkun's son had touched down in New York and spent a week there, then took a bus to cross the country. He wanted to get some idea of size and landscape. He was meeting up with friends in Yellowstone. Somewhere along the route, he vanished.

When word came, Vidkun flew to New York. The police showed him a statement, allowed him to speak to a witness who'd talked with his son, seen him board the bus. No witness could be found who saw him leave it. Vidkun searched for him or word of him for three months, took the same bus trip two times in each direction, questioning everyone he met on the route. No one who knew the family believed the boy would not have come home if he were able. They were all just so sad, my brother said.

So often over the years when I haven't wanted to, I've thought of Vidkun on that bus. The glass next to him is dirty and in some lights is a window and in others is a mirror. In his pocket is his son's face. I think how he forces himself to eat at least once every day, asks each person he meets to look at his picture. "No," they all say. "No." Such a long trip. Such a big country. Who could live there?

I hate this story. Vidkun, for your long-ago gifts, I return now two things. The first is that I will not change this ending. This is your story. No magic, no clever rescue, no final twist. As long as you can't pretend otherwise, neither will I. And then, because you once brought me a book with no such stories in it, the second thing I promise is not to write this one again. The older I get, the more I want a happy ending. Never again will I write about a child who disappears forever. All my pipers will have soft voices and gentle manners. No child so lost King Rat can't find him and bring him home.

Acknowledgments

Most of the stories included here went through one or another of my multiple workshops. I love workshops. One can never have too many of them.

I have a beloved workshop in Davis, where I lived until recently, and another in Santa Cruz, where I live now. I attend, irregularly, a workshop in the San Francisco Bay Area. The weeks I've spent with the Rio Hondo workshop in Taos and the Sycamore Hill workshop, now in Asheville, have been among my very happiest. Going at it, hammer and tongs, over issues of voice, plot, authorial intention, text and subtext, prose and politics is my idea of a good time. The list of co-attendees over my thirty-some years is a very long one, and I thank every one of you.

Special thanks though to Sycamore Hill. Most of the stories here made their first public appearances at the Sycamore Hill critique table. I owe those of you with me at that table not only for the careful and sometimes crabby readings you all gave me, but for the weeks of conversation and the years of friendship. I owe you for the stories themselves, many of which only exist because you can't go to Sycamore Hill without writing one.

Publication History

These stories were originally published as follows:

"The Pelican Bar," *Eclipse 3*, 2009
"Booth's Ghost" appears here for the first time.
"The Last Worders," *Lady Churchill's Rosebud Wristlet 20*, 2007
"The Dark," *The Magazine of Fantasy & Science Fiction*, June 1991
"Always," *Asimov's Science Fiction*, April-May 2007
"Familiar Birds," *Journal of Mythic Arts*, Spring 2006
"Private Grave 9," *McSweeney's Mammoth Treasury of Thrilling Tales*, 2003
"The Marianas Islands," *Intersections: The Sycamore Hill Anthology*, 1996
"Halfway People," *My Mother She Killed Me, My Father He Ate Me*, 2010
"Standing Room Only," *Asimov's Science Fiction*, August 1997
"What I Didn't See," *SciFiction*, 2002
"King Rat," *Trampoline*, 2003

Karen Joy Fowler (karenjoyfowler.com) is the author of five novels, including *Wit's End* and *The Jane Austen Book Club*, which spent thirteen weeks on the *New York Times* bestseller list, was a *New York Times* Notable Book, and was adapted as a major motion picture from Sony Pictures. Her novel *Sister Noon* was a finalist for the PEN/Faulkner Award, and her short-story collection *Black Glass* won the World Fantasy Award. She has co-edited three volumes of *The James Tiptree Award Anthology*. Fowler and her husband, who have two grown children, live in Santa Cruz, California.